Memory at This Speed.

DATE DUE

GAYLORD			PRINTED IN U.S.A

Jane Miller

Memory at These Speeds

NEW AND SELECTED POEMS

COPPER CANYON PRESS

Publication of this book is supported by a grant from the National Endowment for the Arts and a grant from the Lannan Foundation. Additional support to Copper Canyon Press has been provided by the Andrew W. Mellon Foundation, the Lila Wallace–Reader's Digest Fund, and the Washington State Arts Commission. Copper Canyon Press is in residence with Centrum at Fort Worden State Park.

Library of Congress Cataloging-in-Publication Data
Miller, Jane, 1949–
Memory at these speeds: new and selected poems / by Jane Miller.
p. cm.
ISBN 1-55659-118-7 (paper)
1. Title.
PS3563.14116M45 1996
811'.54 – dc20   96-35615

COPPER CANYON PRESS
P.O. BOX 271, PORT TOWNSEND, WASHINGTON 98368

CONTENTS

New Poems

Many Junipers, Heartbeats (1980)

The Greater Leisures (1983)

Black Holes, Black Stockings (1985)

American Odalisque (1987)

August Zero (1993)

Acknowledgments

NEW POEMS *in this collection have previously appeared as follows:*

"Which Religion Vouchsafes" and "Image of a Saint," *The American Poetry Review.*
"An Eye of a Queen and a Testicle of a Bull," in *Shenandoah.*
"Early American," in *The Iowa Review.*
"Far Away," "Separation," "Las Diamonds Are Una Chica's Best Amiga," in *The Colorado Review.*
"Adventures Aplenty Lay Before You" and "Though Not Admonished of Your Intentions in Words," in *Columbia: A Magazine of Poetry and Prose.*
"Phoenix," "Possession," in *SF Review.*
"Flames Light Up the Rough Walls and Earnest Faces," "O Pioneers!", *Prosodia.*
"Far Away," *Best American Poetry*, Scribner's, New York, 1996.
"Separation" and "Though Not Admonished of Your Intentions in Words" in *Voices on the Landscape: Contemporary Iowa Poets*, Loess Hills Press, Farragut, Iowa, 1996.
"Las Diamonds Are Una Chica's Best Amiga," "Early American," "O Pioneers!" and "Possession" in *Contemporary Arizona Poets: An Anthology*, University of Arizona Press, 1995.

Grateful acknowledgment is made to the editors of the following magazines and journals for permission to reprint selections from:

AUGUST ZERO by Jane Miller, Copyright 1993:

American Poetry Review, American Voice, Black Warror Review, Cream City Review, Denver Quarterly, Indiana Review, Ironwood, Kenyon Review, Ploughshares, Provincetown Arts, River Styx, Sonora Review, Volt, Willow Springs.
"Countryside" appeared in *The Pushcart Prize, xx: 1995–96*, Wainscott, New York, Pushcart Press, 1995.
"Adoration," *Best American Poetry*, Scribners, New York, 1990.
"New Body" appeared in *The Key to Everything*, St. Martin's Press, 1994.
"August Zero" appeared in *A Year in Verse*, Crown Publishers, 1995.
A broadside of "New Body," designed by Clint Colby and Charles Alexander, was printed by SUN/Gemini Press, Tucson.
A broadside of "Innocence" was printed by Karla Elling of Mummy Mountain Press, Tempe, Arizona.
In "The Poet," certain architectural details have been rephrased from *Re(Building)*, Daniel Solomon, Princeton Architectural Press, 1992.

AMERICAN ODALISQUE by Jane Miller, Copyright 1987:

The American Poetry Review, The Agni Review, The Antioch Review, The High Plains Literary Review, The Iowa Review, Ironwood, Open Places, The Paris Review, Partisan Review, Pavement, The Poetry Project Newsletter, The Sonora Review, Tendril.
"Memory at These Speeds" and "Tilt" in *A Book of Women Poets from Antiquity to Now,*

Schocken Books, 1992.

A broadside of "Intestine of Taos" was printed by Mummy Mountain Press for Arizona State University by Karla Elling, 1986.

BLACK HOLES, BLACK STOCKINGS by Jane Miller and Olga Broumas, Copyright 1985:

"She liked to be in the middle..." in *Womantide*.

The lines "periplum,/not as land looks on a map/but as sea bord seen by men sailing," are reprinted from "The Pisan Cantos LIX" in *The Cantos of Ezra Pound*, Copyright 1940 by Ezra Pound. Reprinted by permisson of New Directions Printing Corporation and Faber and Faber Ltd.

"There's a song of privacy..." in *The Wesleyan Tradition*, edited by Michael Collier, Wesleyan University Press, 1993.

THE GREATER LEISURES by Jane Miller, Copyright 1983:

The American Poetry Review, Crazy Horse, The Iowa Review, The Nation, The Seattle Review, Sonora Review, Tendril, The Virginia Quarterly Review, Water Table.

"Three Secrets for Alexis" appeared in *Hard Choices: An Iowa Review Reader*, University of Iowa Press, 1996.

"Black Tea'" appeared in The Arvon Foundation Poetry Competition Anthology, 1980.

MANY JUNIPERS, HEARTBEATS by Jane Miller, Copyright 1980:

The "Nettles" sequence originally appeared in *Antæus*.

"A Winter of Love Letters and a Morning Prayer" originally appeared in *The Agni Review*.

The Antioch Review, Crazy Horse, Columbia, Intro 9, The Iowa Review, The Mississippi Review, The Nation, Ploughshares, Anthology of Magazine Verse and Yearbook of American Poetry for 1979, Woman Poet.

"May You Always Be the Darling of Fortune," *A Year in Poetry*, Crown Publishers, New York, 1995.

"Red Hills and Sky" is the title of a painting by Georgia O'Keeffe.

I would like to express my gratitude to the Lila Wallace-Reader's Digest Fund for a generous award of support during the three-year period 1992–1995, an award which altered the course of my life and work. I would also like to thank the John Simon Guggenheim Foundation for the freedom I had during 1989. I wish to express my appreciation for two fellowships from The National Endowment for the Arts. In addition, I thank the Vermont Council on the Arts, The American Academy in Rome, The Wurlitzer Foundation of Taos, New Mexico, The Michel Karolyi Foundation in Vence, France, The Tucson/Pima Arts Council, the University of Arizona, and the Western States Arts Federation for their support. To Doris and Sotiri Haralambidi and to Helene Sauret, my thanks for the living space they generously provided in Greece and France, respectively, during the writing of *Black Holes, Black Stockings*.

I acknowledge, with gratitude, the kindness of Edwin Honig, publisher of my first book, and the continuing support of Sam Hamill and Copper Canyon Press.

To my friends, Olga, Jorie, Barbara, and Jacqi, my appreciation and love, and to Kim, my heart.

To my mother, Florence

and to the memory of my father
H. Walter Miller
1913–1993

New Poems

Early American

From Brazil to Miami to a roadside motel to a super billboard

above Vegas's Stardust you are in vast spaces

at high speeds all watt & animation

your enormous corpse must be seen

as a moving sequence

inflected toward the freeway

received by approaching traffic from a greater distance for a longer

time & may it be known

you take the sign away & there is no place

this being your civic duty to inform us

we ought to have put together an allegiance of tribes

& swept down on the fort & spilled the Christians

off the continent's edge

We pass through town toward a rendezvous

in a hard shell with a child's face

eyes closed straining martyr-like

toward pleasure out of reach

we're in a dying year

no one can take that from us

you leave us soon enough

an autumn to receive gifts

to break the heart

a great blue heron & white goose

to you we are more savage

than the dead enjoying a triumph

of mists at dawn & dusk

the pale hands of our brothers upon us

An Eye of a Queen and a Testicle of a Bull

We each one wear moccasins & a strip of deerskin

that passes between our legs & loops over a belt in front & back

we load packhorses with blankets powder & lead

a bag of meal a bag of salt & a little jerked meat

to provision us until we shoot a deer

anthropomorphic & zoomorphic figures in a dream

we aren't afraid we always fight when we have to

still we feel killing is a terrible thing

do they give the same object to both men & women?

in this time we are going through together

none of us likes to hear folks tell us what to do

& how to do it I hope personally me & trouble

aren't likely to run into each other

we notice an absence of foxes on the present day

young lovers this music helps us pass the time

maybe I ought to learn the blacksmith trade

we never get over our Quaker bearing

I have heard they don't give the same object to everyone

some they kill straightaway

I keep forgetting our house burned to the ground

the narcotic world caught between reflections

if we should live to be very old

anthropomorphic & zoomorphic figures

on an enchantment of islands

we stand to make a heap of money selling land

a city of emotion materializes in tectiforms

we start down the path to the woods

to examine the mysterious fire

but what if we do get the same object?

there is always a hierogylphic wilderness

in which it may be said living is hard

loving an enchantment of islands

Which Religion Vouchsafes

At the end of emotion & description there is a village

there are marriages & funerals there is a trailer

someone without capital works away

half-hidden in the immense open range

a wedding Ford streams crepe paper

flashes & toasts lift the parish hall

nearby a stream waters small fields of beans

onlookers in dressclothes waltz the school gym

self-conscious fabulation on fabulation

one-story adobes with two or three rooms

pitched tin that shines in the sun

long front porches

when they leave their houses they keep an eye out

for stray hens or for dead cedar for post

what I have seen almost everywhere corresponds to the earlier

& true time one has no right to claim

the consequence of this is the only possible one

it is possible that another person is born

of tenderness & fantasy

institutions which daily battle for dominance

at a cattle roundup & rodeo

the value of which is not to be looked into

at the other end of the street screams a slaughterhouse

no one ought to breathe a word of it

free from images & determined solely

by structure the thin white bark of a sycamore

tenders assignations as befitting the time & circumstance

scattered throughout ranch country

the amorous spaces must be seen

as dreams bound & consumed

when they can't sleep they go out bareheaded

for a cool drink

as apparitions who know carnal love

Possession

Again the shepherd in solitude crosses the deformed desert

his spiny head & floating ribs

swaddled in robes

what if the King is dead

what if the Queen is sexually reticent

& someone has said to their child

– shut up, you look stupid talking

by now we are many hours into the night

deleriously happy between the two points of a journey

– I

say it

– love you

so is it now we feed the mythical bird earthly beauty

a thing one never gets to do

twice like a first kiss

eternally green those red hills

I climb

how poor I am

how thirsty & small

the pipeline through the desert a rip in my face

delta-winged plowshares begin a reclamation then the worst –

God is fanged shitless

while each waits a turn to drink

since we deal with life

the potion I-forget-you I-kill-you etc.

don't laugh at my timidity

from scum there's caustic soda there's chlorine

there's copper

there's a little girl peeing

everyone believes she's the beloved

a face with a large forehead

cracked nose & stretch of sand

thousands of wells two miles deep & pipeline centuries long

uranium lead salt dredged like a forced smile

then the worst −

saying to a child shut your mouth, you look dumb −

until now I had not lost the bright colors

& immodest homes of my youth

I care not for images I miss you

all the world's

eternally green & I ask

what if I die without your love my rattlesnake

my restlessness what if I'm buried

thinking of you holding your eyes

with mine then the worst −

you're beaten up

by now we are many hours into the night

pennants of gas fires brighten the skies

then the worst – dark stupid voices raised

painted voices –

Far Away

there is weeping as is customary and good

the lively sitting on boxes

inside the complex overlooking the bridge

I shall have to sacrifice

one of my few intakes of air

to drag him into the coffin room

and choose the right oak come ye

hear the weeping in and of New Jersey

the chosen bent earthward ransacking the woods

unprepared for the tide and wind

until I am like unto him

American Jewish prosperous and free

except for death the freeway below

blasting and blowing us senseless

over a meal mud-tongued I pray

his soul be blessed and returned to work

so that which is decent and innocent

shall not be torn from me limb by limb as I dig

deeper into debt and longing and thereafter

despair holy the father and memorable

his merciful acts of the hearth and household

laboring fruitlessly in the unstocked

and when stocked uncategoried warehouse

the Bronx of our sorest complaint

who shall be judged according to his deeds

his thoughts and his offspring o especially

those stock phrases and incantatory lines

we represent on earth as we are in heaven

rotten little verses transformed by the decent

the good and the young into hymns

of detonated twilights along toxic shores

innocent songs about nothing nobody

who lived nowhere and had no neighbor no

lover no children no poetry

O Pioneers!

Massive rock head but the guy's eyes dart

like cars racing the water's edge

right and left flash the gleaming corneas

of the wolf just as you remember Mussolini

smiling counting off twenty shots

into a policeman's kiosk on Via del Whatever

and the girl looks to be

eighteen is twelve none of this made up

all of it twenty minutes ago

the shooting the embrace the robbery the divorce

the monument to them and the aerial ballet that

leveled them the criminal and girl

iconographically strung across a bridge because there isn't land

to explain their unhappiness

as the water underneath has no explanation

cut short damn it

love is a steep fall from your perspective

aimless harmless but from mine grim and grim

the wide spaces the swashbuckling energy

toothless now and tasteless that cowboy that showgirl

America's triumverate him and her and

me/you inheritors of the latter day

when your amalgam of discrete enthusiasm

settles into sexual fantasy and stereotype

indeed settles voluntarily

what then on Via del Whatever and on Saint

Street it's not a design it's a feeling

that you've gone off on a long trip

with an incision in your rock head

and a dart through one eye though you haven't known

her for long not that that matters in love

God turned to follow your small figure

with encouragement by the light of the moon

to live off each truth

a marriage a crown and a wallet

each tall grass a cry and starlight a rock

with a brother and a mother like yours

our voluptuous words hang volcanically

seven balconies face the sun in our tragedy

forty-three daffodils preen in the hills

we don't see dying

The Unveiling

Wind stirs the gauze from the stone

      and we see his Hebrew name

didn't you miss me

      before the service is done

my mother far grander than ziggurats

      my brother deeper than caves

and I am called

      to take up the speckled pebbles

I bethought myself perhaps the skin of

      which served to secure the veil

it is we who ought to think only of love

      until he now is fully revealed

of night itself that doesn't depend on a guide

      Hyman Walter

the same crowd that a year ago prayed

      not for me to do wrong who never did right

at his burial now summers again

      rash in pressing for consent

by his side crying openly those few

      in a mystery which seems to threaten

some union and shows how deeply I brooded

      weeping very clearly finally soberly

life which you thought you'd give

        everything to come to find out

you resist everything for

        children of the mourners at the site

in a mood which broke up our evening

        run and sing for his pleasure

why kiss me lightly at your stop and not linger

        the rabbi winces as a jet lowers to La Guardia

my case was this and anyone may judge

        father whose trust suns the tiger lilies

whispers in my ear something about the blocked view

        we stroll around and around and I fail to alert you

the family has lunch at the Seville

        where you're from where you're going

we lounge over a meal because who knows when we will ever...

        the thing you find so precious is all over town

Fish in Chains

Along the Hudson across Manhattan to the Triborough

past Belmont Track and you are buried

why then walk me to the lobby of the hotel

around midnight with your having to work early?

it's not that I mind small talk in a coffee shop

not used to sleeping alone I stalled going up

the loam of Long Island ought to have held

well the dwarf yews at the headstone

clay toughened from the record snow

Broadway after the curtain lit like noon

why your patience with me in the theater

my back out? in the first perilous days

establishing relations with you

in this city piled against the sky

at the museum show you seemed bored in another world

and not even on my knees in a jammed restaurant

could I charm you into fingering my hair

breathing in your lap giddy smelling your soap

What has become of our enemy

who hugged the coast for forty days and on

Holy Thursday made port in the shelter of a reef?

Cortés asked where they came from

"Culúa" they said "México"

the next day the first treaty of the mainland was signed

what mysterious diplomacy?

peace fashioned gold animals

coronets some masks and smoke

out of God's hands until there is not one grain

left to put into the ground

why hang around your horror with the body

if you don't know life itself

is heavenly? I stand to lose you again

one weak kiss and a wave

this way you finally trust me

to love you unpossessedly

it nearly rained that's what people had to say

Adventures Aplenty Lay Before You

I cannot know what an innocent I am

letting you get to a new world first

for truth to tell the life's gone out of it

thicket razed to the coast

motels by God bus fumes

but you're desperate time is of the essence

now that it's exactly a year

every day in fact seems exactly a year

to some of us but nevermind

dead a year and still scrutinizing my motives?

though you've barely given us a thought

it cracks the skull around your heart

a gourd as full of seeds as a forest

dear father of bear and deer

You would like to move right

into the heart of the wilderness

because you have the hunter's eye

"Oh there will be fighting all right" you said

I remember you pushed your foot

through one of the burning logs

I wait all morning and not

because I think you'll show

you're fickle and I'm not available

I have another life suddenly your clothes

render you skin and bones

you're a ghost when we embrace so it's torture

like the luxury of showing me the sea as a child

too cold to resist

Though Not Admonished of Your Intentions in Words

Soft thumps in the earth as you approach

you need comfort and food now your body

saved for the time being

trenches are dug under the wooden walls of the fort

that one may pass in and out

fiery arrows dart from the cliff across the river

men familiarly torch roofs

no sooner do you beat the fires with wet skins

then the fire rains down again

the cattle drink the rain

children's hair beaded with tears

a whippoorwill calls

a fish hawk lodges in the top of a pine

the dead live in the wild

hitherto I was prevented from observing

structures burn to the ground

these were events of a time

I went without you and came back without you

by and by the tempest spent itself

I allow that I'm not myself today

I slip my arm through yours

though no one ought to open up that country

first the settlements and claims

then the same land sold over and over

it's at this point in our history

we cannot go ahead if we value life

that turns into tribute

no longer visit my love

Separation

Well my Cadillac now that the hog herding has begun

        big ones spray-gunned

is this the permission we long for

        not in prose or stone but in action?

electric-prodded out of the pen backed into the bloody aisle

        pigs chew pigs' tails

whack the metal feeders charge the gate

        so it's beauty in the end we were after or serenity?

slapped on the rump shoved at the truck

        who shall not ever again find anchorage

never feared July never feared June

        every one with an inconsolable mother...

My ballast

        I've scratched a key along the side of a white Camaro

in hog heaven the place one finds

        community possible desirable

my legendary embankment

        I will never get over you

I cruise the high-pitched scream of the engine

        my tenderloin my tetracycline

I want only to illuminate a tiny thing in a coat

      woolen cap and rubber boots

marked by a spray of red paint

      just where our lovers die

Las Diamonds are Una Chica's Best Amiga

Are you not that stray mignonette of my garden

that dog that prowler in ripped jeans

discovered by borderguards

all mixed up about God & firing

rabid up from Tijuana breaknecking 1-805?

O hogback ridge upended

rock carved by river in air o speak again

granitic angel why this choice

to fit a shape to suffering?

Poets who make it to the traffic are free

to expose their bodies

the haunch of the road is dusty & drowsy

bougainvillea in the cliff's ears

It's a pink shirt it's a hot day

civil authorities drink iced tea

with a cup in the v of their legs

& a bullet-proof vest

they roadblock two miles

shooting without fear

they'll pile-up cars

Why not die as you intended

gas clouds over Paradise?

shock-fronts of amputees

retirees & songs for thee?

why not die under the split in the moon

we've come through?

a whiff of aluminum escapes city center

a whiff of aluminum settles its ounce of vapor

San Diego once beautiful

these mountains moved

dawn & dusk in the transcendent sun

where we are made to die only of love

but who will live this if you die on fire

whose vaporized metal will this stony site be

over whom air-balloons strafe?

Mark how the seashells find their way

to the mountaintop once again

there's an end to this world

scaled down to memories & dreams

be at home in my arms

Flames Light Up the Rough Walls and Earnest Faces

With none among the travelers about you

to exchange words with

you hurry though it is foolish to do so

doors ajar windows open

the lake the pond the sea the dream

the organdy tablecloth unfolds

you hold up the matching napkins and open

what you have washed ironed folded and refolded

out of respect away from the crease sixty years

steady again our silver chalice infrequent guest

lower over the stemware reflect in the pool of

spoons now you would have and illustrate

the significance of knives oiled and of the clarified

vases and of linen finished in lace

under no inspection but the moon's

and return them to the wicker cage

fronting the mahogany hutch

you whitened to assuage the fashion

little else in the home is gilded

two painted mallards stare past their frames

above the radio assaying one another's

round brown eyes and brown and white feathers

in this condominium constructed by indifferent men

with indifferent plans wither not nor weather nor wear down

the single space it has no significance only that

the young mind recuperating language

which repeats without adjudication

shall have none of it and eventually best you

ghosting your watery shoulder

a little chapel in a housedress of windless pink dawn

Image of a Saint

Many favor sunflowers seeding

I choose two lovers late September sharing sorbet

one can always choose to imagine

their fingers through each other's curls

without an image

of their heads bleeding & shouts all around

unnatural lighting & sour air

no small wonder there are deep voices

the wonderful red tiles of the South

an opera in the courtyard

& someone will be responsible for this

muggy lavender field

of vegetal & hay light climaxed in storm

& the stone towers too those

years vanished in an afternoon

the bronze figurines on the door to nowhere

someone remembers them

conjures rows of citizens before the campfire

pig blazing

All these days I've thought of myself

as a poet there's that halo

around intimate matters

in language where impulse rules

intuition too has a habit of romancing

before it's shaded & twilit

as the slow bellow of afternoon breathes

in the shadow of the Duomo

we drive our daydream around

switching up narrow streets

a light rain breaks in on the fortification

heat mingles with evening

the world is noble & familiar

Language is barren before it is toned

by diction & syntax diction especially

& then meaning

musings amusements & nuance

create by the momentum of play and thought

feelings & settings

I feel for you

at home or away whenever

a century or a day goes by

as a creature of love speechless

with no other place to go

at the time we admit it

we ourselves are admitted

into the soft landscape

I study every day & fall behind a cloud

The cattleguard of the invisible ranch opens

a fringe of piñon & juniper stirs along the canyon rim

alabaster cows float in tall grass

cornstalks & sunflowers look like two-pump gas stations

a torn billboard in the middle of nowhere drops from sight

you halt before vertical walls of red rock

the tops of cottonwoods trade birds

Eveywhere we've ever been

children & chickens & bells

the dew of the valley rises into stone streets

drawn uphill to the central square for the day

the squash blossoms of summer have their long nap

disrupted by a motorbike coughing & clanging

an age of brilliant spring greens burns into weeds

you walk in sandals unimpeded

Many Junipers, Heartbeats (1980)

Fragments for My Voyeuristic Biographer

Write that I started in Barcelona
straining against a man on a balcony
Tell how I heard fears on the stair and devoted myself to them

Write those lies because no one is interested in formalities
No one will assume that the stairs were uninhabitable
that the blond man and I were never intimate

Go ahead say I was perverse
letting the others whisper in hotel lobbies
while I went upstairs to finger the spices and ivory

All right I was there I extracted confessions from young women
I stayed in bed all day and listened
knowing I was mistaken I was vulgar

I touched them only at twilight and only because when they left
I was indifferent
I saw their damp eyes their apartments I underwent terrors of lucidity

Imagine their long hairs wiping my back
their nervous kisses

I tell you there was nothing worse than their genuine shudderings
their young lips

Say what you want
I was morbid I was intelligent
I leave you the fragments the furniture the horrible fatigue

The Glass House

I enter at dusk.
The glass shakes in the bedroom.
It was there we all met.

Mother is dead, she is busy.
Father and brother play cards.

Every so often one rises
to clean the bay windows.
The house rests on a body of water.

I enter at dusk.
The glass shakes in the living room.

Mother is eating stale bread.
Father and brother on their knees
eye the precarious water.

The bottom is blue.
The truth is evil and sensual.
Every so often one rises.

Mother is breaking the rock
into sand, the sand into beaches,
the beach into property.

I pick up a rock.
Not that, she says, anything but that.

Red Hills and Sky

My grandmother is dirt and I am desert.

Dusk. The datura unnerves me.
I ride out to violate the baked earth.

Hear the gray sage, how its hairs bristle in wind.
I know distance is a woman I must cover at night,
smoothing her clay shawl.

I ride with my angry kiss in my mouth
until I am forced to stop:

red hollyhock against bright blue larkspur,
tell me who has not been quieted by this.

One Radiant Morning

Like a smile breaking over teeth,
the teeth of an approaching horse,
one radiant morning
a train from Paraguay arrives.

Girls emerge, a whirling of paper skirts.
Not the sun
but pink itself in their cheeks.
We sit in a café across the street.

The clock is not ticking, we think.
We hope they'll enter the park
and lie still in the rosemary.
It's delightful to be shy.

The bells ring, one for each jealous lover.
It's our lives we exaggerate, our misfortune
we watch converge on the square.
One hot day we discover a sombrero full of longing.

A drop could change everything.

Blue Nude

Please take this shy Spanish girl
whom they say you resemble
and ride with her, here are the field poppies
damaged by night, here your blue slumber, your horse.
Take this prayer, which you must surrender
in order to understand, as in moments when you are reduced
to the truth. When you are ready,
the beasts will be there. Let silence go through your heart,
the mild horse your blue one
already stirring toward morning, where it will be white.

Under the Zanzarière

She put the comb in one hand and with the left waved. With that
deliberate ambivalence I've come to hate. The slow kiss which lands
on my face like a wasp. It began in childhood. Mother desired her
and they spent hours together. If not in the garden surrounded by
dahlias and clover, inside the musty hallways or under the zanzariére.

They very deliberately excluded others, though I should say they
were kind to me. When they bathed I listened, not to their laughter
which in itself was omnivorous, but to the splashing, the pauses.
I had too much respect for Mother to be surprised. For example,
her choice of linden flowers for the bath.

They went on like this, conspicuous in the dark. They would brush
each other's long heavy hair. Mother was terribly young, but not
at all innocent, as you must realize. Once, on the terrace, a
liana plant straining toward light amused them. She let Claire
eat its flowers.

The thought of them upstairs in their horribly white chamber, with
late afternoon light, disgusted me. I began to study insects,
collecting their persistent voices, like whispers in another room.

House with Yellow Smoke Sonnet

Two daughters who seemed to be listening.
Was I the mother, was not this
our house? Nária half-slept
seeping out of a nightmare
like yellow smoke. Beyond that –

was it cold by the lake today?

the chill of this child
whose star dazzled elsewhere –
ash. I had to go without a single light.

May Claire's hair be down, may the lace canopy
never entirely cover her most perfect
quality, ennui.
                    Even as she sleeps
I trespass, counting the lonely mansion railings
of her spine.

Lies

Probably no one noticed the mornings I disappeared to sit
in the trees. The light swarmed my face while I recited
sonnets, each last line forlorn but with a tooth in it.
I felt like God, only smaller, flailing my body in and out
of the upper twigs. I lay in a spider's hammock,

the deafening noise of the leaves like Claire's eyelashes.
We were never two sisters sleeping uninterruptedly. Larvae
in their cold dresses. The tree dragged me down against
my will. I ran my hand defiantly through those leafy under-
arms, like a bar of soap in the mouth of a child. A lie

is a cold hand with a light on it. It smacks the cowardly
yellow chrysalis and all the little enemies spill out, all
the little mothers and sisters.

Sculpture

If there is an end
to the sadness of mothers, sometimes it is in summer:
a few couples pass with their arms around each other....
Wait! I want to say to them, *stay*. I'd rather have them
a long time tempting me with their shadows
than a daughter stalking the halls
trimming my heart out of our portraits.
The other child, angelic
encumbrance whom I asked to love:
I too had a summer but scorched myself
in front of its paper landscapes. Almost ghosts,
the trees responded, though only a few. I lolled
all day at the window, insubstantially
over her. No one suspected
frustration, my bride,
whittled my sleep with a rasp.

Spiral in Vermillion

after Hundertwasser

Sometimes the fog submits to the lake, the lake
to the sky. Nária, I loved your sister and I lived
like a yellow sailboat circling
that won't last. Astilbe, paper flower,
                              my foreign girl,
my rendezvous was not with you. Sometimes the innocent
get snagged while floating down a canal
in autumn, concentric, the thousand windows
in red and green, until the gold leaf

itself stops, realizing that hope
is something else. Veiled morning,
contemplative sky. Now, down,
                              why crouch
if not to leap to your wild horse –
auburn, rippling gratefully, relieved
you have arrived.

5.

In this chapel those who kneel are bigger than those
standing, and those who bow down stand gigantic. You
delve deeper into the dark at first and panic, but you
need to *know* all the same. Otherwise how many years pass

like hummingbirds forced to fly at glass? The ivy
fields, red, gray, and the brides in them want only to sway,
to serve the music from the chapel, the chapel far now
from the sea. No greater than a shell,

the soul is distant and within reach. From the opening
strings the white meadowsweet, eyes who never close.

7.

The beeches are vibrant because there is black
in them against the horizon. Hundreds of calla lilies,
the sun's fingers nudge the wide-hipped clouds. Here we are

summoned into the world: I pass those whom I pleased
out of disdain to create, what, a style? And those
sulking, coaxed by the beech in full bloom. The bark

was written on, names I can't remember. How long
is your hair now, how long will it be? Hang discretion
and its three-cornered nuts! I love you and vow

I'm no longer idle, climbing a long line of beeches
like lace. Jane with sunspots; with, almost, grace.

May You Always be the Darling of Fortune

March 10th and the snow flees like eloping brides
into rain. The imperceptible change begins
out of an old rage and glistens, chaste, with its new
craving, spring. May your desire always overcome

your need; your story that you have to tell,
enchanting, mutable, may it fill the world
you believe: a sunny view, flowers lunging
from the sill, the quilt, the chair, all things

fill with you and empty and fill. And hurry because
now as I tire of my studied abandon, counting
the days, I'm sad. Yet I trust your absence, in everything
wholly evident: the rain in the white basin and I

vigilant.

Self-Contained View: "I am a Woman,"

I said. I was drunk. I sat in T-shirt and shorts and basked
in the illusion of time to myself. I had a great figure
in clothes where my small scars were hinted at. People watched
as they observe themselves sometimes, say, peeling an orange,
o isn't this sensual they think in an adult circumspect way.
Lips are popular. We groan into their part, that russet
brown, o o that russet that, ah. Once in South America
someone screamed eat me in a respectable hotel lobby. Oh those
Spanish boys knew what she meant. In the elevator. I have to

prolong this because women like it that way. Only three men
have ever spoken to me about failure. Inside my hazel eyes,
blue and green flares shoot off, impossible to detect unless
you love me. And didn't everyone then: drinking warm Bordeaux,
I held their hands. So many insisted on being included so
who was I to renounce them. We make ourselves sick. I was
drunk when I arrived and am cold now. So little of me is
destructive. We make ourselves live.

Not Ever

So hot so early. Gold light thrown onto the water to feed
little animals on their backs – a dream I wake from to a warm
autumn day. Dandelion puffs and flies crowd the air. Horsehair
and apple-smell. There's an ache in my back and neck and still
three cords to stack. Rust-coppery leaves crack their spines.
Stark blue days, reminiscent of Greek dawns: harbor light, the un-
divided waters – think of it! the variable waves. Fantasies
lace low tide where pairs of lovers bury the past in blond
sand. Because if the universe contracts, it hasn't enough mass

to begin again. The million suns painting Spruce Mountain
circle and hold at my window. They break the rules, they enter
the room, gold-leafing my oak floor. The other day I decided not
to have children. Not now.... *To shut out the light or let it in*
as I please. But I miss their talk, a language I hear as a breeze
to ruffle me. The sun easily hides behind a cloud. Little animals
on their backs hate the coming of winter. They scamper suddenly,
those that can get to their feet.

Immaculate View

love: the power of lust turned generous, the power of sleep
to enter dream: who has not wanted to climb on a warm
day up again toward those sunny hills: remember, how
the whispers sweep us like grass fires: there's always memory
telling our fortune, with a purpose beyond the telling: to pearl
the grainy black day with color where all things long to persist
in their being, as in the beginning: violet cumuli gilded
with lightning, creating space for us as we advance: to think
something never before possible, pristine stone, menhirs,
telluric shocks, daylight earth: o visibility, white as warm
quartz: I sleep and sleep and my father rows out at night,
who taught me, not in pleasure alone but with a kind of fear
to touch another's body: tangible and liquescent, true, un-
tying the scarf from my eyes: what it's like in the void, fierce,
defiant, sad saraband: not with fear alone but in a blind
of pleasure to touch a prescient body:

Green of Mildew and of Verdigris

Phosphor of night-cloud, old salt freighter
sailing between sleep and wake

what was it
you said we couldn't be
eternal about

Summer leaves
hitting the window
undulations with gold-dust and brick-dust

yellow of field and fence
days of October lily
nights of algae and thrush

How animal
human eyes are
putting the ceremony back
where it belongs

Love is the best of the legend
part of a dream we live
beard-of-a-bald-man night
heavy with particulars

and russet days
whose every minute is the same
small explosions like good-bye
so that you will know me

Daily we bury the body
whose heart hasn't felt
each boat depart for nothing
sails of metal and file

On a sea of hinges
we stop our grief in the middle
to work, what we are here for

very mouth, very window, very sky

Troika for Lovers

His gait is like he's got a cricket in his shoe;
he's lost his morning-coat.
The odd one is Mandelstam himself
laundered with a queer name in his tale.
It's the spineless and heroic victim
of *The Double*, Dostoevsky's own
equivalent for Gogol's civil servant.
They claim us in their common round
like song from a Victrola
against the beefy railroad prose
which shuttles generations
like Jews from one zone to the next.

We strut Commercial St. to see *La Cage aux Folles*,
male lovers triumph over a cultural official;
nonetheless, his daughter marries their son.
We're alone in time.
It's our human gait.
On the beach a father taught his boy
not to catch the lines flyfishing.
Sand forms and unsettles like soldiers.
Movements may not thrust
opposites together, but a man with a strange ear might
rest his sunken face perpendicular to an era.
The sunny war lyric of Theodorakis
you honor in you new art, synthesizer.

It's a simple enough act, to bow a cymbal,
if it occurs to you
as music. We empower the odd

number we couple in, three,
cacophonous and far from the possible
which was limited and contradictory.
Men complete themselves or live on
animals. The orderly and familiar
sea drives the new gravel to lyric.
Full moon over a fast ship.
Sometimes it's as close as a string of sleep in the eye
no one else can remove, and as silent –
tradition, nothing in itself
but the dream that produced it.

Metaphysics at Lake Oswego

Dawn like never before.
Rosy bands across bare trees.
For the beginner doubt and possibility both
cradle in the pink sky,
like the beginner empty and ready,
as if an egg under each arm
and without breaking them.

Ada rows out on the lake, oar-plash and bird-call.
So much in love with the music
she just moves, that's all. Great hips!
From the shore you're familiar
with her look – you must change her
focus to see your human face.
Cradled in a boat her body

confirms destiny, already out this March
starving the deer, demanding
you dissemble and bow down
and to whom. Ada in a boat, Ada
on the shore, in the waning days of your twenties,
Ada bathing. Your whole life is overcoming
the past which is fixed

to repeat. With a kind of innocence
rustling the underbrush
you'd crawl from the spot,
red ant toward the real trees,
were she not always undressing
there before a swim. Dawn
like never before charges up

in you, alizarin, perfect and wanton
with something to express, not figure out.
You are here blindly
observing gestures again. Only when they ricochet
do the lights riddle your body:
dignity, hope.
You neither let go nor withhold.

Three Secrets for Alexis

Eliot's lesson from Dante
that the poet be servant

not master of language
that he attend craft

and stretch
his emotional range

omits how to
begin the awesome

first draft.
Here technique

and emotional veracity
count but

like young wheat
we care less

for an act of mind
than a good

wind and countryside.
Birds pipe supper

and through the note
pleasure somehow

translates.
Good and good in itself,

I have two lovers,
one slower than summer,

another like a sea comb,
empty and full.

I hear the old
habits of speech, for ex.,

in this country we say no
for yes

we bite into a taco
at the same time

slugging a beer.
Alexis,

eyes dreams lips and the night goes
was Pound's only line

I heard for years
because in heat its meter

undressed me. In empty space
magnetic fields exist

for no reason. How to use ideas
while living

a line, happy tension!
Quail, a missing cat,

a downpour
and two hailstorms

in one day are equal
access to knowledge

and join writers
in their separate mornings

in the beauty of an act
you spoke about,

placing a candle in a tree.
Light

in a gravitational field
falling turns bluer,

the spruce's new needles
greener

for a poem in the form of an ax.
June, July, August

three secrets
whose time we use

as in sleep
differently to imagine

our sprint and the thrush's
fear when the tree falls,

your idea
about the candle catching fire.

Black Tea

That wedding song keeps thrumming in my head like Da Vinci's
star of Bethlehem and other sketches for plants
must have, a hundred notes on where the forest meets the field,
how the stone thirsts as if it were another being,

and your eyes that change mine in the twilight and the dawn
we confused it for. It's a secret love, and I love
standing in this field, a happy person in a field like a sweet legume
on a tongue, a kiss spiced in rain.

You could be the future because I don't know any better. Ten years
ago I was twenty-one and thought my body was something labial
or palatal and someone would say *silver foil* and make me over.
You're young and can sleep

with ginger and gardenia flowers around your neck and I have to
believe you because parting is the younger sister of death
Mandelstam said. On that reprieve to Armenia under the unobserving
stars for the last time no one knew his name

was under a stone already white with a mushroom's velvety grave. *Go*

for it

the gold in his tooth said, *go* demand the dogwoods
for ten days. Damn the spring that turns to winter again, o permanent
green grass, that turquoise of your famous eyes I eat

like a cow a horse an ass awake all night, following an idea that pours
over me ice and Russian in origin. Your husky
voice ratchets an opening into a monastery, a hive with octagon
musculature. Could I take it in my hands, could I

memorize the whir of desire in this field where the tides have traveled
as if by wildflower, if by chance I could keep what for you
was a given, what for you was a simple thing, how would I settle again
onto the earth, who holds me like a child so far out

on a limb that wasn't made even for a bird. Love more fragile
than subtlety breaks habit; the natural breeze
is your hair across my back and I might have something to do with it.
The night is clear and imperfect.

Some say the stars milk themselves through the boughs of the bare
trees, and some say the trees are never bare. Some even
that these whom we counted on to remain around us like mothers,
that they aren't there. It's a good night

because you were free with me, because you let me cry on your gold chains
that led to my village. The two of us up there
for a look, you know the place where the sheep are born
and the goat milk is fresh, with you it felt like fruit

going back and forth across me on a silk boat, your eyelashes
suddenly bare and a message, the song
that tensed my neck with its I'm-not-a-child-anymore teeth, steamed
into worlds of wild honey. The gods are in the leaves.

Immense Virgin Girls

Open the door where they knock sighing.

It's a humid receptive morning.
All in voile dresses they enter:
a receiving line of obsessions,
twelve sorrel horses.

They puff their gestures of regret,
sorry they aren't marmalade,
though they are, nor sponges,
wet with consolation.

Why do they breathe together like a bouquet?

Why do they amuse themselves
with mother-of-pearl necklaces?

Where did they sleep
that they awoke so many memories?

Why, with violence,
do they throw off their pretty wreaths?
Twelve offers and not one would renounce you.

Look at their tender repetitions,
the blue eyes of their reputations.
Immense virgin girls!

Infrared Meditation

Body and memory, poles linked in rapid succession
like a woods by gunfire, by a fire sweeping just shy
of the search. Fire whose aura is a mirror of travel,

our moment of doubt, red leash on which we pull and catch
glimpses. Here the invisible, here the red squirrel was.
Glory of the fire so black at dawn, so tempting by noon,

stroked by evening. When we walk back, there are cold thighs
and the sun setting flames on the far eastern hills. Dogfights
spot the warm snow, bitten ears. And you only felt pleasure

without passion, only remembered the lily flung down the spine
of the terrain as accident! Hateful to talk about exploits
like a dog: the only beautiful things are prompted by voices;

one acquiesces or fights. Called down the dark slope, you
have to make a lifeline out of a few flashes, glow and after-
glow, body and memory, what survives your spirited sleep.

Steamy Meditation

Canvas houses vent the cat-like peacock's *shrill*. All
settle now into the vaporous night heating its vial
of iridescent rain. Salt cache, salt belt of heat, virgin

island. Lizards, one learns, are good for killing
insects. Mosquitoes fester where we piss off the porch.
Pure eddying waters of memory, Proust, the yellow finch

who sips at our ears during naps. Underwater, the feeling
enlarged is the feeling. The last days of childhood I biked
in our basement where blue skies ripened at night. Sex is

the scorpion who disappears between floorboards to live
again as a god. Pressure in the inner ear, my self, to
steady the bike would be to steady a wave. Seas crossed

by winds turn the curving patterns we perceive, probabilities
greened. Rain and angels partly explain the parting sky.
And the waterfall turning to mist as it leans.

The Sparrows We Weep We See

Driving for hours
and still morning: the princess's white undergarments!
It seems we were the only _____.
Imperceptible is the soul

coming to request,
like a lover
in you as if to find the smallest star
for which the constellation is named:

Lorca somewhere else,
sun going-down-like
on a woman rolling
my eyes back, fucked
by tongue,
the secret-myself-away, though there are names for it
and tensions turn that way.

Having fallen, not in English, no,
the petals tear, the sands, uncomfortable, tilt,
and the scents and dusts burn unnoticed.

Burn.

Black sun, yellow rocks, sand, no,
black rocks, sun, yellow sand...
strange, monumental,

a day of
look, trees, clouds, sky.
Whitecaps stop 200 yards out
and apron a sound like the lagoon opposite,
its slavish rocks holding unsteadily,

doing their jobs poorly and giddy besides....
One sail, birds soaring of a piece,

how many birds?

thank yous,
the partings we call joy.

Tulips for Two and Four Hands

boats an alphabet in the canal
something painted in our name

a few prostitutes
who? I thought

mannequins at first
knees bent

horses working
the streets steamed

like a night bath
or a poem about smoke

moon and icicles
or a photograph

some with your fear
giving way to color

have faded
as when you said

there's nothing like the truth
to open the evening

we have separate lives
even turned

toward you
let me

see behind you
the raised slips of the waves

    .

far from home with its small
'm' one could rest on like a loveseat

the endless water that surfaces
from below land

disappearing and being reclaimed
the tiny music of ships in bottles

what Braque calls
the fortuitous

all of us versions
virgins

loosening and losing
to the thirst of the salt

like an island in my flesh
I remembered

being shoved into a lake
saying *gallop gallop*

and slapping my heart
the same that thanks

the sides of cows in this dairy region
a distant part of me

catches
on the milky stars the ritual

carving of the blond heads of cheese
your homeland for the first time

surrounded by ideas
Hart Crane accompanying himself with shipbells

some on the other side of this world

    .

as we took the curve
north across a few bridges

a narrow slat separated
a village on stilts from the sea

bicycles slept openly
signs disclaimed about the morning

sale of truck-sized wheels of edam and gouda
out of place for a time

like evening in white-face
and seventeenth century dress a couple

huddled and trained to the edge
as if they were the foreigners

as if there were someone
I could trust

to say these things for me
and we were the secrets of families

a pack of dogs
out God help me as I have always wanted

to imagine the dark green lining of the moon
once we got it in sight

.

it's only paper-folding
for beginners the season shuffles

its coarse hairs and wire
Dubuffets sprawl outdoors

the pond a plastic
reflection and shade

I test my head on the head of a Buddha
you focus and kneel

our faces in the tulip fields
in our cups in the restaurant

thick with lipstick and rouge
a few Van Goghs we'd never seen

his unfinished fit of blue and azure
his hospital

the simple balconies covering with snow
the urge to build

peace out of time
so what if I'm one figure

being woven on a loom
brushing the blouse of the weaver

the desire to take you
the humor of mobiles

the utter fairness of glass
this music of the rocks

barely all my life
as the first star is scout

into the night like beads across the abacus
stretched out even willing

from Black Holes, Black Stockings (1985)

COAUTHORED WITH OLGA BROUMAS

Enfleurage

As from a water lily, *periplum,*

>*not as land looks on a map*
>*but as sea bord seen by men sailing*

successive ferries, my toy boats, leaf, song, heart. Or again, I step into a street and, commensurate with its width its bazaar breaks into range, wares, voices, steam float distinctly in unequal units closer. A blur of relations and then synchromesh: rachet, whistle, bulk, cold, scallion bitter, fish heads, city dock. Out of the midst of the city the country, forested one by one into many, alert like the tops of trees with inexact news about an imminent arrival; I tilt until it becomes time and there she is, most beautiful come upon from behind, where she is waiting for a moment, discouraged her message never arrived. And as she turns, her sunglasses glint and she brushes back her braid where her hair was loose before, and since; there is no one of them that does not see her, unconsciously – and, white birds casting a dark shadow, fly out of themselves.

We parked and hiked and climbed over the wide sleeve of the Atlantic. Below and between, the beach where even in season the many travelers rested or tossed far apart. In perfect September I sent them to be alone. Without mission or admonition. Feeling as we did then about each other, already relaxed, how would two wed the fall of summer, speechless for three days, how far from the other? Satin shorts and roller skates at night in the streets of the village, transvestites. Perrier and pistachio. The fabulous dark divulging day, deliberately provoked. Saran wrap and plexiglass about the night and the day, the membrane between them. I thought we might lap and here at the great magnet meet. I unmade my bed, wind torn from clouds, massaged by distance, and slept. We pull on cords from the earth where we are joined. We the plural.

She liked to be in the middle. One of them was taken by how close her heart beat to the surface like a robin's and how she landed with a light touch. If the sheets were white and the sun glanced on them, blond had more red. Another was olive with almond eyes, who liked to wake slowly and fall back. She lay beside the row of windows and rolled out into the night on their long wooden oven spoons. Sometimes they came for her and woke her, kissing the corners of her mouth. The long hairs in the bed, the very curly, the weighty and the subtle, lit an arabesque. When they were wet they were very very wet, and when they were dry they were funny. Excited, the candle burned like cry-breath. Who called out and where answered and when became thirsty. She reached for the lucky pitcher sailing across the sky. Tissue, tissue, kiss you.

Four kinds of song, at least – sweet, insistent, erratic, shrill; and hare traversing the thorn bushes that would berry. Butterflies paired, almost clapping to their flutter; and the rustle of olive, pine, and fig. So the porch overhanging the valley signaled the hours with its players. Time rounded into a sun who appeared to stand still, then flattened to the horizon, became measured and horizontal again like Euclid's geometry, explainable. Matter, at a perfect temperature, a certain mood, dematerializes before us, takes on more than its qualities and, irrecognizable, we say it disappears. Love, calling itself into being. Or the dancing bear at the end of a pin – happy relative molecule. A haze of heat, an idea, a chance meeting, color. Made of mutually exclusive vibrations each with its unknown, its irreconcilable heartbeat, insect-whir. We traveled here and arrived after. We play a duet and don't hear it, hear it differently, hear it later, heard it somewhere before. The heat, the song fills us, therefore we say we are hungry, and we uproot the lettuce at dusk. "Lettuce," "dusk" – they mean something and are funny, a sort of a song.

Lizards and ants yes, mosquitoes and flies no. Yellowjackets yes, wasps gnats bumblebees no. Nightingales, swallows, woodchucks, dragonflies, fireflies yes. Myna birds usually. Kittens, puppies, guppies; pigeons, doves, yes. Owls, not usually. Nor do I like dogs in packs or frog-singing, mating in the fog with his camouflaged baritone. Buggers. Do flies bite? One mother is a bitch and the other pink and pert. They were here for a performance and tea, mothers of famous lovers. Serum is squeezed out of a bite, not without pain but the itch is gone; makes a funny mark where you've bleached your leg hair rather than shave. We all sang Try A Little Tenderness. Risk of pus. The countess invited her publisher and one mother a series of relatives. Split genes, clones, insomniacs, reptiles no. Fly-by-night, tea-for-two. One sang for mother, another recited. Goods for nothing, good for nothings: one loves two who loves three. I took each Polaroid into the sun: the countess and mother-in-mourning are dark against the great blue; the other mother and the countess again, impressionistic, fleeting; a third, of the four of them: daughters and mothers who had been – overexposed in front of a bowl of wild strawberries bleeding together a little. Looking up I saw out of place on a fig tree limb a rather large mouse staring down the fabulous blouses of great beauties with a secret, mine, happy no matter, pulling it off. We spent the last hour of the night, at last, just looking at each other alone.

Of those we have let go – those shy to scandal, those of your country unwilling to forgive your exile, the almost-as-famous, the nostalgic, those who accelerate scandal, those willing to forgive, who hold to blame as to a leash but are the dogs – how many of their departures do we still suffer under a different name or delusion – the need for reward, the calamity of competition, retribution; in the morning light, the tamp of plastic awning and in the evening clack of roof tile, the living we divine by *imagining*.

She rose from them, walked through the room, at the door, bowed, and turned. It was her opportunity between formal goodbye and exit to judge the impression she had made, a demilitarized zone in which she was already assumed gone. Bowing, she kept her eyes up to fix the panorama and trick an accidental gaze into a matching bow. Taken by surprise and politeness, invariably he smiled into her closing eyes, eroticized, in her favor, where she left him. She had been presented by the minor official but it was the general with whom she had slept a month ago and to whom she had addressed her request, without looking at him in either case, the latter according to his preference, the former hers, as in wearing her hair severely back and off her neck – having discovered in a similarly critical situation with a gentleman of means that one is seen and not recognized if a great feature like the hair is hidden. And turned in her handwoven silk scarf embossed with an ancient script without a word, having chosen the few necessary ones which had been repeated twice, once for the general, in the straightforward manner he had asked her once for a certain act, and the second time that the general's audience might take in her beautiful white skin where the royal blue kimono cut away. An ivory sash swung at the slit if she gestured, which she reserved for when things were going well; they had. Her lover would be released from prison where he had been detained five months earlier for contraband and was sick from claustrophobia and filth. She had been allowed to visit him and was given a handmade Malay suit as she had been given her impeccable manner: from the poor, who accepted her generosity of spirit – and money when she had it – returning abundantly like the beloved silkworm.

O restless one, who climbs to the top rung in the rain and slips on the last dowel, searching the far hills for morning in its yellow slicker; or, on the way home at the dinner hour, late autumn mulch smell in a gust with evening-roast, you take the wrong turn suddenly into a thicket; the stray dog there, his snap, and the eyes on a tree trunk with coarse brows; a creak; a cry, yours – covered with a quilt in your sleep like moon by fog – wrestling the hammer of the woodpecker out of its parody of your heart; and in a sweat throwing the cover off now, freezing the cat on the sill by dilating its gold eye with the one of yours whose door snaps mistakenly open on its crusted hinge. Sleep shapes the pillow of the weary and infirm, of the one woken by rain, and of the others in thought and in love, turning. A rise of late moon chafing the sky slips between earth and a few stars, perhaps the one you were dreaming of or, through a closed lid, projecting from; therefore the disc must be rolled away with an arm as if across a dark sheet. Inertia squares itself, yogic, and breaks you almost into consciousness to budge it, falls into the perimeter of the circle and tumbles in its moon finally away from you. Heavily the magma of earth's core shifts, throwing a few warm coals into your hands; and then, because you have sunk so far, rested, believed, you reach the fires kept burning. And burn your craft there, waking.

There's a song of privacy that begins Go away Go away, and stills the mice and the porcupine too, crouched at the door as you fiddle the keyhole. Lizards, asleep, roll a little farther from your bed, spiders hand over hand in the moonlight climb as if to it, holding the rim of the amber pot until a signal to scale down again. Alone, alone, the sweet golden beads with their interior lights guided by destiny guiding night travelers beyond, back or askew into the not-here, the knot in the crossroads where they must tire and halt like a girl caught in her hair where the teeth of the combs are too tight together, throwing the comb down and sleeping deeply on the tangle, worsening it, happy in dream. Tomorrow it will be snipped away, tomorrow the porcupine will startle you from the fig tree, pointing its tears at you or, worse, beyond to some backfire or allergen thriving among the geraniums; snag, broken egg, broken string. But now the silent choral, the poppy growing sunflower-size in a vibration Chagallesque, tipped in flare burning in, tranquil candelabra with its funny rhyme glowing inside you.

They would send her to a hotel in Barcelona if she couldn't stop her moods. Anyway she spoke Spanish, with the good humor of one who has also studied Chinese, with a flair for its pictorial and lyrical quality. The contemporary version of her love of the classical guitar was the jade-inlaid electric she got in Hong Kong during a brief port of call. She was on the boat as a last attempt by her family to purchase her education; therefore the world. She was seeing it through the eyes of kif, those pearls that made her blue eyes gray. She carried her perfume with her like a veil, lacing her scent with American designer kitsch that, mingled with her skin, turned floral and impregnable. She attracted attention even when she was too inexperienced to notice and fail to dispel it, which she later learned by observing others do badly. With a languid mouth and quick step she would fly across the room and smoke with her back turned: a habit of hiding her nerves behind a blank expression that made her look younger and would be good for at most another year; already it was incongruous with the abstract beauty of her face filling out rose white, and rose red where the small scar on her upper lip drew a shadow. Before their car was found by the police she searched the old city in the deep purple hue of her jacket and of the dusk it never failed to signal and illumine where she hurried. By the sea at this hour she heard the song that eventually made her famous dimly chorused in the waves, in the underwater of the mind darkly, purposefully. She hitched home by the coast route to find them in bed, back from the police, annoyed at having had to leave their address. I was happy to slip the curtain of the street from her, the intoxication of her future made more palpable by her failure, which afforded her distraction, resolution and charm. She gave us half a sweet laugh, the half that is at herself.

A gram. How much?
Are you married?
Yes.
Is she?
Of course.
Where are your men?
My husband is arriving later.
Will he let you go?
Of course.
Where are we going?
I will meet you here at 4 o'clock.
How much?
He will let you go?
4 o'clock.

In the film version she writes across his forehead in lipstick MINE. We drank cool liquid out of Chinese decanters at the villa under its long beams, under the overfed moon. We kept the inside cool like a cave and, very sober, waltzed to Vivaldi, missing the minor tones. I took her on the white wool rug protecting cold stone, two unmodified extremes, black and white marble. We were interrupted by a family, a husband and wife and wife's mother, to whom the house was to be shown. Had they not seemed tranquilized we could never have avoided being in the same room together sharing one blouse. Having come to say good-bye properly, the other, different and equally undemanding, never even saw the inside of the house. She drank three glasses of milk on the back veranda, peeling the croissant crust off the chocolate bread, and asked us to lie in the grass. For once the sun was directly overhead, neither casting shadow nor, where it did make shade of the overhang or leaves, distorting their proportions. We were one mouth unadorned, making an imprint. As lithographic ink is black before it is receptive to any other color, the most moving operation is that of the almost complete effacement of the first imprint.

Women who fly on separate planes to meet in strange cities, poppies with their black follicled centers, chicken eggs with a little blood on the shell like a stain on a sheet, the stain soaked through and left on the bedpad unwashed, print housedresses washed and, in the wind, torn at the hem; pneumatic alliances: the plane too low, a drinking glass pitched off a table, uncracked, but with its blow to the head, unmarked, bleeding inside a drop; bird coo, too regular, parrot trained to the French national anthem, bumblebee, its lion markings burned black, stabbing the window and otherwise horrible fly. Brain dust, spindletops blown in the air, brow furrowed with electric violin practice, seeds planted too close in a furrow, tomorrow, because of a dream; giving orders; taking orders; the wearing of black, the wearing of mirrored glasses; dust; haze; ants on a naked woman, lipstick on a man; with a penknife, manipulation of a developing Polaroid; periodic rinsing through the night of the menstrual sponge; the days and the nights sulphuric between golden and leafy, between the sun and the moon: discharge, between flights in an airport: dizziness; black, yellow, red; yolk, ink; the beautiful striations after the sun sets invisible, as without love.

the only cool day of summer
kids at bullfights
yellow and purple
green olives under an almond tree
a trapezoid smile
indoors without a flash
two aunts and an uncle
avocado vinaigrette
a bath with no hot water
a spoon and a fork
illuminated hands of a clock on its side
the hidden side of an arriving train
Paris at night
a face appearing at different windows of a big house
the last half of April and the first of May
one other

She whispered *anemones* naming the flowers the boy had brought, a minor scene against the erotic masterpiece of the girl and her older lover Brando. We walked in in time for and accentuating the suddenness of their first intimacy in an unfurnished apartment. Driving home, after the movie, people we passed almost knew what they were doing in the back. The sunroof was open on the powdery sky and the narcissus from Tangiers smelled differently on each. One wore it like a light laugh surprising the air, the other like a vapor. I drove carefully exercising my hearing – I loved to hear first and see later and later still to touch. Taste, the darling of life, lay on her rosy couch on the other side of arrival, where we would fall as into a great beginning elsewhere, after acceleration, after light and sound. First it was like talc and then oily. I let myself take in from the back a finger, and there the darkness of all our colors lacing the room quickly magnetized in one spot like absence focused upon and enlarged – light, lightly. I was disappeared into an impersonal moment where the casual is sacrosanct; that anemone, for example, into which I was driven and from whose center I was pulled, into time, rested, ready to sleep.

Melons best and then berries. A city where anything was obtainable and people loved, because each had come from somewhere else, a variety in which they were represented: linen, silk, good cotton, and how these steamed in our salt in summer. The cry of the vendor, dry, foreign, announcing, on the last of the vegetable trucks, reptilian cauliflower, beans, and the powdery peaches whose undersides held the shade of the Negro hands which had cooled them in the distant South; creaked down the burning street, this mechanical horse, and was unburdened. Rubber, asphalt, concrete, stone, wrought iron, brick, the substances first introduced to a child as color – sienna, mahoghany, Indian, red oxide, blood, vermilion, carrot – and then as solids, the verticals and horizontals, the flat and the stub one bruises against. The tunnel to the park, its cosmic fluorescent; the park's climbed trees, the secret hiding place in a small boy's neck: tunnel and tree and humidity. Mother lifting the moon out of its brown-paper sky and easing the knife through it; and the knife wet with the small hairs of the central sponges – but airier than sponge, like the pliant night sky with its air holes of star – and the light would break the honeydew open at the last second so the two halves rocked on their ocean floor. The juice shimmered as the child balanced on the side and gazed into it as into a swimming pool. Sweet there and safe; cool. Four asleep in the one bedroom where the air conditioner beat. The floor all bed, the sheets ironed with a cool palm, the palm on my back rocking me in my sea-body.

Blue of rainforest green, of moss, ultramarine of closed eyes, evening pearl, berry black, blue of earth cerulean in space, royal, prussian; porpoise blue and whale gray, slate blue of metal, enamel; iridescent trout, blue of fungus and mold; sky, pacific, mediterranean, aqua of translucent blues, blue stained with yellow; iris, silver, purple, rose blue, military, grape; in the shadow, violet or port; pool blue, quivering; church-stain, red madder, octopal; ice blue; blue of sighs, bluebird in twilight with a white stripe; polka dot, blood blue, nordic, light; diamond, meteor; parallel lines, density; powder, red, white, and blue, blue concerto, island.

To have by heart a complexity beyond mind's intervention, I lay a curtain over the bird-cage brain, open to the close world of the ant, how it scurries with its meal the size of its head! O improportion, towel mountaining the surface of the hot porch the insect must traverse, especially as I step, making out of a foot a black cloud out of a blue sky, the sudden dark of one of you going away, going away. Followed, fallow, fuel, we are star between earth and nothing blond graying into white. In the background someone is always knocking hard on the door wanting in, unable to imagine what takes so long, who goes so far, which one of them, a triptych in the Chinese vein where seasons are simultaneous. There was no name for it, pair and odd, pair and odd, or did I dream you there, song of my region? The words anybody can use them, ΣΤΗΝ ΑΚΡΗ ΤΟΥ ΣΥΛΛΟΓΙΣΜΟΥ ΠΑΡΑΜΕΡΑ ΜΙΑ ΛΕΞΗ, turned on their heads side to side. Pigeons like roving seashells on the *quai* talking as fast as a Parisian. The caption-making intellect among the floral postal cards, a vaseful in the city, a season in Provence.

Your aunt's daughter married a diplomat, the perfect setting for her having been raised in several languages. The children now added Spanish and Portuguese to the list, and spoke these to each other at the dinner table, gliding their feminine endings under the Arabic and French. I was remembering how a left-handed person ought to manage the fish knife beside the easeful manners of the children. The German asked about my work and his children followed my English, the language they liked least. We thought about being sorry for not having changed our dayclothes, not when they asked their daughter to curtsy but when she did it and remained mercilessly untouched. We thought it would ease her release later for her mother to have excused our freedom, thinking the important fact would have been that we knew how to dress with our money, like her. We saw the snapshots of Buenos Aires and heard about having to hide the Mercedes and use the old car; not stepping out at night – that they had to be fortressed he saw as a mark of distinction, as he said with some pleasure. Everyone ruffled at the table except the aunt, who was loved, and whose reasons for being pleased that we had brought flowers were insignificant beside the first one – they were simply beautiful.

The very perfume Kienholz must have used in his environments on the 1950s – the slow music, the polyurethane men at the bar, or servicemen in the waiting room of a house of prostitution, memorabilia about Eisenhower – all on a brown and red carpet of roses. Your mother's letters at your bedside table, unopened, overpower the wilting cherry reds. She follows you to Europe with her drawl and plaint. I practice the flute, cascading cheerful melodies with low notes on the end. The Festival, the tinsel, the flash of light in the eyes of the well-known and us, driven into the event by your departure. That day we heard of the terrorism and shootings and were sorry we had believed you were going for a rest. Not that you would be involved, but that once there would find con- sort among those wronged. We surfaced among costumes on the promenade, the faces of the hotels marking a period of history when architecture was sculpture: colonnade and white facings below black ivory domes, crystal high in the dining rooms' omphalos. We drank sambuca under the celebrated sky, blacker and more riddled for your absence. It was your drink, and we sipped to the hard coffee bean, split like a nipple; we were surprised – very few people had heard of it, although it is not uncommon.

I have some snapshots of this coat over the years, up to today when it unraveled, its ribbing caught on the rose thorns outside the countess's door. In the negative the luminous thread repeats the outline of the oriental cherry she planted soon after moving to the south of France and which chokes the anonymous local fruit tree with bloom. The coat is from Hong Kong, hand-embroidered with the same tree, and I wonder if she will take it with her to Barcelona along with my camera. She is now up posing the countess, where it must be difficult for her to achieve a natural countenance as each feels the slight of the offer reneged upon for dinner. She's going to have it difficult where she normally has it easy, as the countess is jerked back from senility by anger and demands much more coherence from her than she, in the drugged mood in which she prefers to work, inclines to. In her absence I watch the rain pool on the porch like the concentric abandon of a delightful idea when it occurs in a mind able to follow it without regard to time until it becomes simple. The hours of rubbing graphite on stone, the lifting of the stone from bench to press, the inking of the block and the cleaning of the ink, the application of the tusche, the moistening and sizing of the paper, the registration marks... The David Hockney print she sent from London in Chinese blue and white called "Rain" mocks my abbreviated days with its long process, his leisure to invent after that period a process for merging paper-making and paint, where he dropped in for a visit and stayed a year.

Like shower over the heart muscle and, after rain, summer. Peaches and rose. A steam bath for the earth, Chinese massage, long silver pins drawn the great distance of daylight from hand-clouds into trees standing on their heads, roots. Waterwheel over the terraced vertebrae, earthface rosé tanning toward the many the long the most generous hours of light that today rain, yet light, the lightest gray, gray apple-green, gray lilac, white. Solstice of pins, of verticals, into the haunches of horsehills. Tongues in puddles. Hours in twos and threes, hours in elongated seconds, thick sentences taut and thinning into words and finally breaking into alphabet, moments without shadow, the long spaces between lights in a countryside going to sleep in even daylight from the rain, and the different lamps meeting in the evening making gold the gray, buttering the houses in small swatches as if they were children holding out their pieces of bread, watching the last light perforate the darkness and not admit to it, no it shall never, happy soul, winter.

Remember how close we sat in Sifnos having dinner by the water? You said in your country once you put the table in the water. You began the meal, and then what a great idea to move it over a little, it would cool you, it was that calm. You rolled your pants to the knee and poured drinks all around, the fishbones back to the sea. Lizards climb the stone outside the kitchen by the sea. Weeds and flowers grow out of the stone; the relatives spill out of the kitchen. The daughter is well-educated or about to be. She serves us with the happy face of one who is leaving. You lifted your skirt walking home in the dark over the pebbles to sit. One night we saw the only other lovers – they were both fair, she blond and he gray – and their eyes moved only to each other and the sea, these two destinations. Now the sea once in a while slips a wave up to their feet, because a boat passes or for no reason, now the yellow moon divides the sea into fields.

from American Odalisque *(1987)*

Sycamore Mall

Coppola's *Cotton Club* starts at Campus Two Cinema Saturday 6:45 mall time.
The Negroes in the film are played by Blacks,
playing opposite the tennis shop, tobacconist, lingerie & antennae sales,
a glass-cased elevator & automatic bank teller.
Because this is a strangeness tendered in others,
a display of the humiliated
& recast human being, a thing Michelangelo transcended by marble
in David with its oversized right hand,

because this is a tenderness strange in others,
I dine formally in a towel with day lilies & hydrangeas on the table,
fresh raspberries & roses in their second bloom,
then sympathetically go out on the town.

Symptomatically it is as if I am approaching the Doge's Palace in Venice
& the piazza is covered with ice.
I exit my hotel on the Grand Canal, Paganelli's,
& slide arm in arm with my lover.

It was right to act back then, in summer, as if I were living
a love story that would be simple, with its curious
nocturnal glow, not unlike the mall hybrid light,
where like a single thought there persisted
an electronic chant on the portable tape player
as from the bowel of the Basilica the choir repeats a benediction.
No one ever touches himself in public, Our Lord,
because we've all rubbed off on one another so much we're invisible.

That is what has become of the tree for which Our Mall received its name,
with hope that it won't be the end of the world if we act out

of our best mood, surprisingly delightful original sex
without climax, a gift reserved for the end of the century
for those who still live by the spirit
of an act, on a street prepped like a movie set.
It was right to act back then, & to trust the movement
of the affair to the relationship

& insist on perfection. It'll be a while
before we are hoisted & joined as characters on a screen in sepia tone
for a theater inside a mall under the influence of temperature control.
Painfully one day we wake & haven't the right
clothes for Venice. It has snowed as it did, we are told, once a lifetime
ago; the full evening moon floods the piazza & in the morning
workers haul benches for the tourists to pass over.
A simple pear from a painting, or the marble hair of the David,
bandages art places over our eyes,

survive in Renaissance books next to the jog & diet shelf.
Michelangelo & Giotto appear naked to the touch,
holier because no one is fully conscious nor ever able
to forget anything under the false light of the dome,
Our Ladies of the Air Conditioner, the Air Freshener,
the Night Moisturizer. Between summer & winter of a given
year, I reflected on life to no end,
& fell in love, ourselves in a lover,
like art whose strangeness tenders a body in others.

Picnic

A mother and child activate the lawn,
the child in her sundress and the woman in white, barefoot.
Their Post Toasties are post-modern.
I sit closer to one of the speakers
that rests on the statistical curve of the backyard,
the long curlicue signature with the dot after it.
Every now and then I imagine
we could as easily have gone for a swim in the rain.
As long as we give someone a window
into our personal lives,
like how I spend the winter
in the desert and the summer by the coast,
somebody has to, then it's somehow
OK to be casual about the narrative.

Therefore casually in the grass
the violets paint the mother and child
with all of nature between them,
a dot of yellow shielding the sun.
This couldn't take place
on metromedia television, because the message
is the corsage the woman has on.
All form avoids recreation.
Memory has to have a good time too, at any expense,
the jerk who asks Who's the pimp here anyway?
and is a syntactic greeting.
Let's leave them alone, innocent, the baby
doesn't have to be a line nor the woman a sentence.
The yard explodes.

Near You are Heavenly Bodies

I adapt the rhythms of my actions to the affairs of the earth
        maybe you don't want to be loved everyday and maybe I don't

is it arbitrary or is it intuitive?
        I'm just going out for a moment

a complete change of life and a profound rest
        shall I remember my beach as one reminisces about fame?

my father's tender direct kiss on the lips
        meaningless in the way someone thinks

I'm just going out for a moment
        but only suddenly

with no shirt the beautiful
        day coming onto night

fear or freedom when that's understood we build
        it isn't a matter of acquiring it's a matter of divesting

who were my friends among whom did I move?
        yellow apples green and red grapes red and orange pears

all I want to preserve is the landscape
        a guy walks into a bar throws down $2 adjusts his nuts & orders

the end of the century cries out
        now tell me did you get up like this at night as a child?

on the pretext night wasn't made for children
        we have to prove we're honest

how did you know I belong there?
        a state as obvious as California

who was I stopping to ask is this real?
        the smallest creatures near you are heavenly bodies

natch! I'm just going out for a moment

Topos

At the documentary level, a voice on tape
survives an instant, chatting about
politics, money and love, then is extinct.
The language is local and commercial.
It fractures a moment. On the screen,
meanwhile, on a darkened nightclub stage,
a star moves. One is not oneself
on stage, one enters an autistic drift
with music. For example, I hear storks
in the background, a whistle, an electronic
synthesizer, a metallic bird. It isn't spring,
but the organist plants seeds. Then I'm part
of the audience.

If I call and the phone monitor is on
they will hear me ask for her
and be able to talk about me while I'm talking.
Behind them is a South American
wood flute serenade. Sounds like wind
through empty Pepsi bottles. Heads swaying,
hands snapping. It's a devotional exercise
and the carnations and tulips in their living
room, couched like talk show guests, show them
watching TV, tourists at home. I call,
finally feeling at home in the motel,
listening to music, wanting nothing of my own,

everything to belong to my mate and my mate to me.

Memory at These Speeds

I love these hours alone I do
               not
                    like them. Like them, I am
slow to divine
                    meaning from change, meaning
I love you & remembering
                         waking next
to you like a white gull against a white sky
                become blue
I feel detached, although I realize
this is the drift of happiness it is not
               my choice
                       yes I like you
for it. Faith
             for this moment is living
with a fear
             I will lose you or myself,
  each arousing
           the other,
eternity!

               that spectacular hour in the afternoon
        when you arrive & suck me
               as if it were through time
we are reconciled
               or in dream,
     the desert we return to
       heaven
            all that disappears
      when we look back,

                                    for this time we are lovers we are
moved by the sea
                        in a studio with aqua floorboards
      & white lamps now like stars inhabiting a pattern
                  now random.
Never let ourselves be subject
                              to either dependence again
or pain. Where once there were so many
      words we had to choose
                        between us,
your sentence effortless as mine is fair.

Tilt

I am on a peninsula
forty miles out in the Atlantic
and have driven my car to a mechanic
to replace its ball joints.
I left it in Wellfleet
and am walking every half mile
and crying and walking every other
the four miles out to the harbor.
When I get there I intend to
pace the pier and receive
the appreciation of the fishermen.
I have a mind to fuck
one for the afternoon.
This probably won't happen, and not
because I'm not good looking, and tender
in grief. Anyway the cry
has become more
like a detonation, dry, brief.
It's all right. I'm not doing this
to forget, and I feel great
humor and communion. Standing on this pier
where my own two feet had been
on similar docks in Amsterdam,
Biarritz, Nice, Athens, I remember my mind
wandered even then
from the two lovers I happened to
have, traveling the sun to serve
our ends. Tomorrow,
why the hell on earth
even bring it up, like a tide

brackish, effervescent, pink,
familial, I'll be back in town
with my freedom to come and go
geared to the misconception
I want to. I wrote a good
friend and fruit grower, Mary Fisher,
a few weeks ago, it's funny,
Mary, I'm on a red bedspread
in The White Horse Inn in America,
you're on the other soiled coast, California,
I'm talking *broke* and more beautiful
than that day you saw me leaving
my husband many lovers back,
feeling rummy. Christ: girls,
art, money, I'm thirty-three,
this isn't TV, and there's a war on.
Do you want to live
forever? Or is that poetry,
a wild iris I was sent,
wasted at The White Horse
powerless to a fault,
one for everyone.

American Odalisque

Schwinn rests in back seat
of my blue convertible;
leaving, I'm sorry.

.

Snails sprawl fine sand, dawn
spills like waste into the sea.
I don't care either.

.

Mobil Station next
rest stop, where I phone my love.
Busy; no answer.

.

Coked & dancing, I
think of Cape Cod now, your voice.
Shivering barstool.

.

I'm safe now in town.
I sleep late with my new love.
Remember? Say yes.

.

Cool, professional,
like a river is a slave
for sun, I seek love.

.

Pepsi & money
flow easy; I need you here
while I am just past young.

.

I stall on the bridge,
press my emergency light.
Berkeley, a lifetime.

.

Midnight. Heaven is
bathing, the window open.
Just a kiss away.

.

Aren't they always
mistaken for images,
your Invisibles?

.

A coyote, bats,
they put me in no mood here,
I can't touch myself.

.

And think of the moon
who is my family since
I have no children.

    .

Are fish unconscious
and mute? Last night I ate one
in lime sauce. Years pass.

    .

My car, your shadows.
Roadrunner skids to the door.
My friends are scattered.

    .

What will the new art
be made of? Dusk, a snowfall,
same cold human feet.

    .

Easter Sunday sun.
Stewardesses picketing
United parade.

The Cover of Mars

The Lucille Ball–Desi Arnaz hour concludes
with a Fix beer slipping my neighbor's grip.
Again he will sleep on the cot in the vestibule
under a pile-up of stars. Now he shouts
at his ignorant self in Greek, and his wife.
Now that I am returned from the taverna
like change from an empty, I lie in the amphitheatric
vibrations of the alphabet of
international report and arthritic snore
pelting the strip of beach invisibly like moon drag,
white on white on decanted white forever,
having wandered out of three ouzos with dinner, wondering
whether peace with the Turks lasts
because war with one another continues
mentally, calibrated astronomically,
whether people's hearts are too sore to care
to reclaim territory, or whether I have not listened
or lived in such a way that I can understand
a strange country's fate, let alone
my own, wracked with mosquito at this juncture
of adult love, from this as from any altar, better
than from the shot of morphine
the doctor administers the last time
I freaked, cramped, I can blame
myself in your presence and claim this room
never had to do with my life, someone's
rotten smiling teeth above an undershirt like sailboat
mirrored upside down in sea, lit in the courtyard
by the cerebral cortex of ultrablue cable television,

Lucille in flames, addressing Ethel's willing
slow take, the enormous wash-out of beach, weed,
sea, sea, and sea, so that I can remember
my center, backyards of beautiful barns and junked cars,
the America I lose you in when we return,
with precision, and with my usual splash
as from outer space, years later, alone, I land
up on a given afternoon crossing
the Mississippi into Galesburg, Illinois, through
Carl Sandburg Drive, past cemented Penney's,
singing down Main with the church
bells of an historic cyclone, as one remembers
an old life lifted from an old notebook, as obvious
as our souls drifting the coast off Mars
or worse, your face on the cover of Mars.
I give you back my heaven. You're all in my head.

Destiny

I am eating cold Chinese
in Joy's friend's flat.

I have been trafficked like a drug
planted by a child in Oaxaca,

like the story you are happy
without me, a lie I believe

you believe. And I am traveled
like the mercies on Telegraph,

the streetlamps burning down
the throat of this thoroughfare in Berkeley,

which gets us off
where I lived in the sixties and now

see my name in a window
and find its theme

useless in the act,
where had I not been

so privileged then
I would have had hope

well-humped for a quantity
of uncut drugs.

Out of the city
on Joy's cocaine

where it's always the freeway & the hour
the bars close & no English spoken,

where men chain to each other
as to an idea, say, that prayer

is as useful as a condom
against the current cancer,

here is the black Mercedes
of an acquaintance, top down,

and with the stars tight against my body
like a drunk I am singing

because in a war you taught me
your people flaunt a joyous will.

You who have raised fairness
to an exquisite pitch

which sounds like the wrong gear,
is it fair

to go on as the everpresent
red light we run

parts its mouth for a tongue,
three queens high on Stevie Wonder

crying *Where were you when I needed you
last winter?*

Now that it is morning
and the only person I know

drives by in his cab,
my name on his red lips the sun,

I call back
every minute the speed of the hours

of the days of summer, *Friend,*
not naming him, remembering his name,

and that's how it's been,
one with the universe,

blanking out at the Art Institute,
an expensive drug,

piano-brained, cleared to black and white
like a spaceship to another galaxy, MTV,

while you are happy with someone
somewhere there

is the same crying and laughing,
two peasants,

the one you are and I become one
day when we aren't dead

to each other. I hear the story
of a stripper from her mother,

how she'd studied with the National Ballet
that when the lights go on you don't

pretend, you're alone.
I love you.

High Holy Days

I am the Princess of Life Gone Out
I am the sunless parallel in the vertical

Two spirits forming out of the quiet by day
& the native by night
Most demure, Jane
most meditative of you

to broadcast the velvet of an inner thigh
of the nymph in the summer sky
& for the last secret effect
before it goes out over the airwaves

tell me something equally heavy
which leads the dancers to the hanging
of their red-hot tights to the line
setting the sun

Now is the time, whichever you like better, friend,
all inferior beautiful thing

Her skin is whiter than milk   her tan is darker than beer
in the shadow of special dispensation
like for a Jew the absolute
saints sighing & fairies crying
all over their invisible members

Random cradle starting up like a life in me
Don't be surprised if I laugh the shore says to the water
every time you win in the end

but live where
since we didn't know of any place to stay
to take in an even smaller part of everything

a case of a sacred object
not making its escape toward evening
a cow
implanted in the video arcade of a Midwest mall

a small head nobody will believe I did it
Saturday night after the movie let out
seized like a biker
with hazel eyes like headlamps turned yellow

If it's such a deep secret no one will verify it

Goethe has to describe the beautiful
folds of Christ's garment
raised off the ground exposing one knee
before we get a sense of internal space

automatic freaks like auto freaks through a wheatfield

In my heart I have a memory of you
but not the brain to decipher it

god the wind as windless as the world behind a computer screen

Out of the air-conditioned inferno in the broad street
high school girls bleach holes in the darkness of Clinton Avenue
I stand like Ozymandias on Quaaludes
missing whom I miss

once in reverence & once in despair I dreamt
we got both harbors

Sunset Over Handmade Church

Like,
people get emotionally tied to
the first person who
fucks them up
the ass,

    god willing,

we were driving toward Biarritz
& stopped to call Alexis,
exhilaration in our voices
as we described the scenery, an emotion
akin to Carlos Williams's
man swinging a shirt over his head
or Hass's shouting hello

                  to an empty house,

& as
the one pleasure of the traveler
holding a lemon to his nose on a windless day

                  is to know he can leave,

the week we saw Arles
we enlarged everything
out of our minds,
Arles exactly as painted by Van Gogh,
the goldenrod, wheat, apple trees,
no one
tending them in all the hours we drove,

for the French, odd,
                        not a soul,

the difference being
we had each other & were still
believing in a god,

ménage à trois, the next day slept between mountains
where the proprietor caught trout
& we ate in the poised and spirited
style of women alone
among men in the immaculate
dining room,
                        like a picture of a country dining room serving rose pears.

What a night in a featherbed
in a room with a high ceiling,
life has been good, good, finding
our empty purse & providing
the wine we drink under a quilt.
                I did not want anyone to see that my face was so happy,

because I had slipped into the face of my dead,
who know so precisely what to relive
with their heads calmed
like a unicorn in the lap of a virgin,
                                & through me drive through France

with you, this mental self who
buys a paper & crosses the square for a beer
in Tourrette-sur-Loup, scaling the terraces of the olive
trees after lunch
                to play the wooden flute.

It's this distance from you,
this freedom we have to forgive,
that keeps us on a tether

                        like goats, exactly like

ghosts.

Ozone Avenue

These days I love to dream,
then I go hear *Romeo Void*.

It's a gentle hell, beloved.
Teen-age boys with lead guitars

singing a number like
there is no like,

you're gone.
I suck the little megawatts of my memories

which are nothing
exactly like mirrors

in a bar in a different mentality,
L.A., Albuquerque, Berkeley,

queens drunk and coked to the teeth
for the imprimatur of the closing

bells. I imagine
I do you

riding toward my fascination
the speedway, and the next minute

the next minute
sniff jasmine no one sees.

I lose the image of myself the rest of the world has
to catch up with. How long are you going to be

the rest of the world? One long day
the lover you left me

for returns to sleep
with you, you can't do it, it's ancient,

like talking
about sex and not realizing the lead

singer has one leg squeezing the other around a mikestand.
Knowledge is useless,

Heaven in script on a turquoise sweatshirt,
with Private Clubs for Los Ojos.

Where is this room?
Just a sweater with nothing under it,

a blanket with the design of the future.
I can see how she is because we only just met.

So used
to living intimately sometimes I wake

feelings in others I don't know.
Mornings the prostitutes

on Mission in halter tops and pumps
ignore me as if I'm just another

voluntary miscarriage of an intellect.
Forever is getting faster,

air
traffic no one hears over a beach.

You make a small gesture on that beach, love,
flicking volcanic ash off a cigarette.

Miami Heart

In a long text, on live TV, in an amphitheater, in the soil,
after the post-moderns, after it is still proven
you can get a smile out of a pretty girl,
after the meta-ritual lectures,
after the flock to further awareness bends "south,"
and Heinz switches to plastic squeeze bottles,
as one flies into St. Louis listening to Lorca's "Luna, luna, luna...,"
beyond Anacin time,
after, God help us, the dishwasher is emptied again,
and Miss America, Miss Mississippi, reveals she has entered 100 pageants
since age six,
Packers' ball, first down after a fumble,
the corn detassled,
the assembly of enthusiasms awakened,
and we meet in a car by the river
not not kissing, considering
making love, visiting Jerusalem, the awful daily knowledge
we have to die in a hospital on the sixth floor, in a lecture, on live TV,
or in an amphitheater at half-time,
at one's parents' condo, over pasta,
in a strange relative's arms, in debt, along the coast, staring
at a lighthouse, the heart bumping, bumping the old pebble up the old spine,
a squirrel scared up a sycamore by an infant,
along this stench of humility, along that highway of come,
charge card in hand,
I shall give my time freely
and the more I dissemble the more I resemble
and the more I order the more I reveal I hide,
the better, the faster
I sleep the more I remember

to go elsewhere,

a movie, excuse me, now I must whisper

not to disturb the patrons,

now I must drive, now park, tramp to the edge of the world,

roughness, ferocity, cannibalism,

bite, chew, transmogrify,

inside the lungs the little revolutionaries, between the thighs the reflex

it's too this, it's too that, it's not enough,

similarly, and more particularly, it's raw twice over,

it's the imagination draining its husks, left-handed,

because comparison is motive, which is why

one writes with one's desire.

Let Three Days Pass

Let the one released from feeling,
merged in the neutrality of doing,
let him be the image of God.
Turn the channel to him, focus,
and let him float across your screen,
allied with mass culture.
I saw it, right on TV, and
I taped it on VCR. The color oozes
into reality even now, at midnight, during the
lightning flashes for which He is famous.

Nothing looks this good but really
the technical imagination makes it so.
Don't you think?
Here's a final minute, boundaries removed
and lightning on the sacrificial stage.
Eternity is caring for others,
the worst winter ever, where one does not exist
in a landscape but in an obscurity

exactly as lousy as the core meltdown
of the Brother nuclear facility. The first
two thousand die right away. And
the others, the Polish schoolchildren on the border,
the Romanian schoolchildren and the schoolchildren
schoolchildren wait fifteen years,
showering every two hours and scrubbing their hair.

Video Rain

I am flown to your good side now.
Hiked up like a skirt,
the elevator intones
the cardiac, the cancer ward,
& finally the stroke floor,
because we're always in bed & need to be reminded
we must all carry our seed in our heads like flowers.
The insane staking an identity on high-tech.

It's time to rethink the entire landscape while I still have the body for it.
After years of doing what you've done, you'd do it too, my hero.
As I drag you to one side I wait for the coin to drop
& the video to begin lighting its commands,

ATTENTION this is your stress test,
having to really give all that suffering up,
having it as a guide, not a destination.
Everything is explained in-flight.
I can't stand these elderly stewardesses,

computer tones whispering FORWARD.
At Atlanta International there's a sharp tear of fluorescence
on a poster baby & in eyes that have just come from the freeway
as from a marriage of Mobil & McDonald's.
Getting off at the right time like a drug,

at Terminal C Olympic games are re-run,
blank sharks the pool, *blank* scarfs Wheaties.
This is consciousness of 5 P.M. airtime,
where temporarily I live

on the corner of Asamblea de Dios & Destino.
There's my exit, low tide, a last morning on a beach, & this is
it, isn't it, the earth we despaired of with Texaco
refineries & acid rain & you're having to take the hand

of the man in the moon, the black male nurse so clean
& necessary. Like tourists reach for a Holiday Inn in the fog,
as you feel for him I have been really feeling this
country lately deciding what to do next,
conscientiously pressing street crossings
like the accordion which opens into a city,
and the only difference is this really happened.
For everyone, Dad, the days are long,
but it seems like we're always in bed,

sunsets outside quiet silent towns.

Peace Lyric

In a dream of sex & blindness,
boats grow rare on a river.

In a meteor shower which I feel but can't see
(as I sense there's something in the future

though I don't feel it),
the tossing of plums & grapefruit.

At the pole dance at Picuris,
a sheep tied to a pole.

At Santo Domingo, dancemasters & clowns attend a line
of elders & children;

a breeze floats down, an elder escapes with a story in his hands & feet;
in the morning I learn who was awake.

Arhythmic beats from turquoise & white deaf & dumb
drums, olive & gold-painted,

dark-skinned, when they rest they rest on their sides.
– & I will be dead, this will have been me –

not to my homeland, although that too, nor a lover, exactly,
nor others surely, nor water & skyline, those too,

but to that absolute lure, intuition,
a coal sunset after diamonds

from the incremental gazes of the maiden dancers.
From the gazes of the dancers,

the laughter of my young lover
for those who want to know

all I will know of having a daughter.
At this altitude

grasses sprout like headdresses on the roofs of adobe, & in them
the dream of a blustery day in a city.

Under the wheel
on the High Road to Taos, deconstruction, demystification, demolition,

the unexpected downpour daily at four or five.
No longer harassed by my passions, hunter yellow & spring yellow,

violet blue, light gray,
there comes to pass like midsummer through a mountain

cheerfulness, sorrow, serenity.
No one go with me.

Lost White Brother

We are about
to move away from guys getting messy
at their headquarters two tables down.

The you is gone, the bar vacuum is on,
the TV turned high,
casting a sunset on the opposite wall.
In the intelligent Taos Inn, a copy
of the historic Ansel Adams photo, *Moonrise,*
Hernandez, New Mexico, hangs.

Like, dehydration city,
like, work, like the spirit ants aren't going to move
out of the bowel of the valley, the ski resort.
If I go home I can sidle up to my bed
and arrange it so I slice the moon on my pillow
for the official margarita of the lost white brother,
hailed by prophecy. Lorca died this same age, 38.
Some people's parents are still alive, and there will be that to deal with;

and I have approached this close like a date, like a feeling.

Don't think you're alone
in needing to be alone.
Whether it's his last egg Mandelstam offers Akhmatova
upon her return, or my beer, my refrigerator open to you,
& you've seen my picture, you know with whom you're dealing,
we are the same lost white other,
obligated to hold the sun up in this culture until it rests

on the opposite wall like last night,
my love.

O'Keeffean

Through the window the piñon
with its precious nut

each which must be picked and peeled
by hand darkens in bloom,

and the old dogs called in
sleep, and the soft adobe cools

by lamp to crimson
and, too, darkens.

I am in love and no one I know
for a good thousand miles.

What the hell,
freedom to scale,

nor anyone to call to.
For months I have lived for the day

I could reconcile my anger
with my wish simply to start over

as your lover. And now with my heart
content as the ancient ocean,

both figured into desert
and alone, I release you as heat

transforms the apricot and peach
trees painted on the desert

of the year I hurt,
each beetle, centipede,

black widow, what I am
supposed to look out for,

like the rattler,
who contains my death

more than any other
I also love and more since

to love is to love the most
feared on this red earth,

with its heaven dark
blue like I imagine the mind

because the body doesn't have to
question day all night

nor the invisible
moon on whom I practice

your face.

Centripetal

This time if there is time if time
embodies a true story, I'll tell you the truth.

So well do I know you
that were I blindfolded and led about the summer beach

I could tell what part of it I was
standing on from the perfume where you'd been,

that olive skin moist like the shore,
as a child the fairest in Athens, up early to escape

to school with your satchel in the shadowless glare.
Go friend. The southwest wind blows across the Cape

with the constancy of a parent, and the heart-shaped
air sacs ripen to iodine and a blackish-brown.

Everywhere the stony smell of dry sand and hot salt grass
should remind you of home.

What I thought all winter were pebbles I see now
are snails impregnated on the rock. I can smell them

three thousand miles away in Santa Fe like the one
thing you can't smell on yourself, your breath.

Although I don't get used to it, I think
of you making love with another with tenderness.

Among ponderosa and joshua, among juniper,
I play the piano attentive to the whole piece, like sky.

The sunset is lavender and gold, equipoised between three peaks,
slate, fire, and pearl. Stepping outside in the ashes

I call in the dogs, and with them a race of gods transformed
to maize gathering the meager end of summer rain.

These obsidian Apache tears I found in Sedona to bury
with you in the East. They say rather than die

by another, men leapt from the mountain weeping these
stones. I know how deeply one can look

into your eyes, and down there perhaps you must be
lonely without me. Among the mosaic

of the Taos range, proud Wheeler Mountain and the Sangre de Cristo
chain, yucca blooms like desire equal to the sun

rousing it. If memory serves me,
I cup your sculpted face and loosen

your hair as you stoop for the bath. I live
the risk of the romantic. Nothing can save me,

who takes leave of you for love
remains.

Intestine of Taos

The dirt part of the road is five miles.
Left up short steep hill, left. Second definite Y
road winds round, road follows pole with two black arrows.
Where there is only one.
The first time you're frightened,
then you can't live without it.
Several windmills confessing *I need you,* once or twice.
But it does not happen twice.
O ocean,
I'm sorry I met someone
when I was with someone else. Straw in the walls

and thunder every afternoon.
When it is noon,
the poor pooling of men in the state penitentiary.
Along the onyx leg of the drive to Albuquerque,
painted cars and nails along the freeway,
lone view, the dirt road and the tiny branch.
But this is not that branch, nor sun in the afternoon.

This is not heat. This is the brain walled,
the church at Ranchos de Taos
exorcized fifteen angles in the sun.
Wind on the corrugated metal eyes, on the hoarse
stalled motorcycles, the motels of love.
On a Saturday, on a Thursday, all afternoon.
Violent beauty, is that what beauty is about?

passed psycho pickup trucks,
a windmill on the right,

this is that dirt part of the road,
whether love,
in certain cases, mightn't be superfluous.
And immediately after that ardor, this technicolor plum
hastened to that dusk, those friends, one other.

It is unusually cool for July, not for a moment have I forgotten
the infinite tiny poem bolting the arroyo,
the fable of the red,
the drench of the white,
the felony of the yellow,
the cleavage of the black

cool summer night in the desert; boulevard of stars.

Broken Garland of Months

After Folgore da San Gemignano

For November I give you the little Latin moons *lunaria,*
       hauling water from town without spilling
       the beautiful sounds of the words themselves, little

moons. May you compose a poetry of the tasks of this world
       in a privacy that is so amorous and does yourself
       so much courtesy, it is like the last great days

of a courtship whose flower always pollinates your wrist.
       In the mist, get a good idea and do it. Inside the
       pumpkin may you carve the flame.

For October I give you all holy the bell of the deaf, bells
       of alarm and delivery, one if the red squirrel hunts a
       mouse, two if the mouse finds a home. One if the chill

sits down at the table. My brow is flushed. I'm wearing
       my orange sash, hurry. Or maybe it's better with you
       gone, a bird who escaped the gaze its beauty invites.

Someone far away has made a decision in your favor.
       Or perhaps it's only kite-play, making infinity's
       sign that the old and the new pass in and out

of each other forever. For December, a hundred-fold late
       harvest, acres with apple and pear picking an hour's
       work, and round about you so you are never weary

dancers for amusement before your every day of study.
    Let sunsets regard you as God's maiden too dreamy
    to go home or on. I give you a lover who wakes

waiting, who lies down beside you and is pasture.
    And who stays up sometimes craning after a few
    fireflies for fear you might cross and not come back.

Sympathétique

The magnetic moonlight
the metallic moonlight
I turn up the thermostat on Dodge
February zero & I down a Special Export
You're out confirming the dimmer switch an all-night light
an alkaline moon a chemical moon

The graveyard stones name several unrelated Millers
three blocks from Dodge I bussed past them in a blizzard
this early evening with the children from the retarded school
down the street the street snowed in like a canal
A case like Van Gogh is impossible today
there's a filter on the sun
the snarled moon the journalistic moon
I am a sentimental lover
who would sit through a storm to paint the horizon
the charcoal moon the whey moon

Driving your car after your evening engagement do you feel glamorous
you are and I can't wait to touch your face and neck
who would lie down and love the earth and the earth tones
your dark auburn hair to the shoulder and your creamy belly below
rosy white
Above all else the figure the figure in the landscape
In church? even in church the figures in church
the potato moon the moon of the poor
Vincent punk Vincent victorious Vincent the bohemian Vincent the great
But I want it to make sense it's about love
I want to announce that each time we go down on each other tenderly
we learn something we

hike out in late autumn or early spring before really
the earth's opened up hands stiff embracing three paint tubes blue red yellow

earth in the cemetery minerals like jewels
and I don't think How bad is the pain?

It's portable it was born in February green red black yellow blue brown gray
The temptation is to stand out in a June rain and enjoy it for itself

from August Zero (1993)

The Poet

You would procure the oil of forgiveness from the angel
at the doors, and get a small branch for a tree
that finds no use until it becomes a bridge over a river.
You have a premonition, while crossing,

about the wood's fate, and rather than step farther,
cross on foot. The wood lies dormant for centuries
until it's dug up and three victims die on it,
scattering the Jews. Unable to discern The
cross from those of two thieves, you place them in the pit
of the city, in the early hours hold each above

your head, and with the third are brought to life
zipping between buildings at high speed, shifting
into fifth out a disembodied ramp.
The thrill in the air is sexual, the ballpark darkened
and the hologram of the shut airport glowing,
your headlamps trained on mall light in fog made
more intimate and infinite by the collapse
of time, cement bits swirling your sealed space
to the strains of violins. It's the dawn of an era.

Time does not improve it. You live in a sunny place
and work in a sealed building. 10 MPH on Interstate 405
by 2000. The twentieth century, begun in Vienna, has ended
in California.
...gas meters on your left and electric meters on your right.
Ahead, at the end of a passage, out in the light
a flight of concrete stairs. As you climb

you see the big towers of the financial district
fifty stories high a few blocks away...

The sense of entering a city nobly, walking the freeway at night
before it's torn down, hearing Portuguese, German, Japanese,
French, Chinese, seeing views of the bay, metallic, choppy,
and of the suspension bridge, and the ships, this is over.
About the demolition, a few warnings, like those about the earthquake.

The clack in the streets of Vienna, a carriage door slamming
and a continuous fountain, though far away, seem no farther
than the broken freeway. The bells of the tower, quiet.
The stones smooth and brilliant in moonlight.

You are in a car with music and air conditioning and a phone.
Softly, the classical station massages you.
You know in the back of your head
the best of your creative life has been siphoned away
by desire and money, desire in general and money in comparison
with others, but between one abstraction and another you yourself
quietly and fiercely participate in a disappearing place,
one you loved and were prepared to enter
with great humility, bathed in tears and barefoot.

Any Two Wheels

Firecrackers thundering day and night, and lightning silences –

a few blossoms, the lowly mountains, that pair in the tunnel of love
                 – and it is a tunnel, and it is love –

it's almost as if everyone is smiling on the streets of the government,
the weeds can touch us only so far up our legs
                where it will be spring, spring when we get out –

easy to live without money, without equality and power
in a bar with a lemon fizz, dancing with the two or three best lookers,
a little older than one might have picked, hippier,

– no, it wasn't a holiday!
       – I only knew one such day in my life!
             – whose fault was it, as far as art was concerned?

the flower that very night I have in my hair, I shall talk about it briefly –
the end of the war did not bring liberty, and that seems to me
more dangerous than pain, my little anacin –

my arm ached from keeping that flower intact, I have quite a head of hair
you see, and a blue poppy is hard to find, really is
a strain on the imagination, no?
– now when the firemen put out the stars I think of it, I

– it showed me how exhausted we had been, touching language directly,
and though nothing is conceivable for us now, the borders
of language fade – film, magnetic tape, mime – if you look closely,
down on one hand if need be, you'll see the discourse there,

                    incomplete, digressive,
the lovers kissing and arguing at the same time, the heat divine,
and as long as time permits, they go on smoking –
                    they think it's oĸ sleeping alone in space –
ascending and descending the misty grapes as if there is no art of
                                              interruption
                    – and they are grapes, and it is misty –
now that everyone loves the taxman and embraces the police
                    whose lips are like berries too,
berries of course are now entirely terms, no amount of
gentility can conceal that fact but everyone is properly
instructed in sheer projection – listen,

a heart this big, if anyone's asking, utilizes
diamond chips, and in the poorest countries, as big as a ball of thread
which sticks to your hand and draws the boat ashore, where a hundred
years are as one day, that same woman weeping since the erection of a round
                                              tower,
                    the first sign of official culture –
– was there a ridge with a lake on either side?
                    – beachfront and pink sand?

the sulphur sets and the sulphur rises like a minotaur,
our bodies are straight and perfect, daylight as black as a beetle,
and white as the snow of one night, all our nights.

August Zero

Young trees the bright green of a moonless night,
lawn the red of scorpion, –

the pleasure dome drops, a drill ceases and a mower resumes.
It hides the spectacle of the mountains
and jolts us, it's been a long time
since we've had a little space to ourselves.

All the same, in spite of everything,
we are made to live in the air, which involves a certain number
of mental operations
the full force of a bow, a revision of the notion
of history,
oddly imitating the movements of animals when I think about it,
doubling back, appearing to be shot or struck –

and celestial sounds, not sound itself
rock the bare earth, packed hard and nailed
to the tune of the unconscious,
which we regret to understand.

Don't get me wrong, there's still a knowledge of freedom,
a bath, a change of clothing,
possession of a child's heart,
a handshake, and the function of time
a detail – even in air
language is a
cross between an appetite and a mouth –

I'm not hungry when I'm lonely.
Like all the lead and neon which is forgotten
I forget that people have died forever,

no one knows you
and the ideal place is a dome with horses' shadows
the shade of steel gin,
and what formerly acceded to a view constitutes love.

A pear –
remember now future became present –
in a kitchen and two rooms in orbit
pins the horizon with its pony body and elk head
and we enact where we first made love the camellia of our beloved –
we can't touch exactly
but attempt a profound correlation –
we grip the skeleton of a river and the sun kisses it
like one's own throat.

This is the earth, my love, all of us
have a chunk on our backs.
You are an angel
and I am an ancient
who're cast from two and a half billion cars a day

into one copter night,
and closure is that windmill
through a wall in the circle, drifting
like the once innocent

oil spills in the Pacific,
like conversation.

Scattered Alphabet

Our initial faith in the world, our father, if you will,
was not true enough –
everything we lack takes on definition and form.
For example, on a hunt for our parent sun,
a whole day, a whole city involved,
there's a sense of overdoing it, a monotone,
and when we find it, no longer yellow – never really –
looking at it, our headache is someone else's

       collapse in space. I cease weeping
in the mornings – mornings are now part of theater –
and when a planet roars by –
              honestly,
space is a world of play, there's no reason
why it shouldn't be – the continents wander like
huge rafts or lava-flows but without danger
of spilling since there's no down there's merely

five billion antecedents. There are substitutes
and assumptions where once there were summers
eating chicken and watermelon.
You are my brother when I write;
I kiss your face.

– when I see you I remember living with you,
      imitating you.

And when I try to dream another world,
a crystal of the continental crust – you can imagine the bondage

of those for whom description is redemption –
my soul dwarfs
                        – I know the future
is included –
                    that feverish afternoon
our brittle father and pretty mother
            marry again,
                            carbonate ooze to monsoon.

Giants

Someone's old parents in the desert on folding chairs,
one cradling his face, the other absorbed,

a Jew with blue eyes and a Jew with brown,
and inside, behind a huge plateglass window,

a modern dining area, black and white high-tech kitchen, swivel stools,
a lot of counter space,

and their daughter basting a turkey with orange sauce.
The father has only this morning

confessed his wife's secret – something he never tells her he knows,
though he assumes she knows

her father – who would be near 100 now – never died
when she was two, but abandoned his daughters and wife

and gave Florence and Rachel – lifted from the Bible – the gift
of the public trial of early sorrow,

which each wore far from her nature like a boxed jewel
that escapes down the throat and illumines the heart,

as the throbbing of the cosmos is lit
by what preceded it.

The man in the chair, whose leg won't work when he gets up,
has accepted his wife's anger as depression

and forgiven her, turning down the light
like an orchard lamp, low and steady, for fifty years.

I know them, I have bothered to inhabit every maneuver
until they shrivel and I am sky that darkens over

them – these creatures in the yard, fallen
like lizards into a pool

without water, gesticulating and blinking, wiry, slow,
whom I let slowly go

into a house, settle in front of the console and press the remote
to each memory station – pause, hold, mute, flash.

Figure

Were we to have invested in a figure more distant,
whiter cities, blacker tides, bluer moons?

to have swum at night
as if it were an insufferable day of shade?
Next year gone, missing,
and the sea that damp paper at the extreme.
One hears of eternity rather than remembers.

Like anyone taken by emotion
and chance, the lace and the ice
mountains, we watched the filings from the night
stars razor-part the foam from the water.
Full moons, high wind,
nothing apart from imagining,
a world reduced to a vineyard
beside a cloudy pool.

Tired of flinging our arms back, our faces forward.
Tired of the dive, the save, the pure
form of the verb purpling the hotel where we collapsed
the language of charity,
the final minutes of verse.
After an instant of fulfillment, where's God?
Experience pressed us like a grape.
After forgiveness, we see the earth divided
because the screen in our bedroom shields the rays;
now I see your face in profile (geometry), your hair
in a towel (allegory),

your lips pressed to mine (surface).
There was a fiery scrub, and we were to have survived it,

the worst of which is the bomb blanket.
As for the light that spills off God's glance,
careful records, faithful studies...

A peach blushes in bright sunlight, it must be morning.
This is the day fondling
the moon's reflection on the water,
tossing it, smoothing its hair,
babying it.

Are we to invest in a figure more distant,
blacker moons, whiter waters?

Screening

A society intent on living in the present tense
likes coming home and doing nothing, but turns on
Entertainment Tonight as a form of literalness,
like seeing someone for the first time
in a photograph, staring at the thing and knowing
our future to be tied to it, shocking, hard to imagine,
hysterically seductive. We don't want to kiss it
or give it a hug, but its presence is purposeful, like a tribe
whose history functions to call our relationships
into question. The situation lacks urgency, yet at the same time
what's public is always so real. We don't therefore have to take
my word for it, we can think of ourselves

as an audience and know all the same we're a view
lit by lightning whose life is imminent, a showcase
of stars just behind what is visible, nothing a small
commercial break can withhold forever.
For a whole moment our lives
are "state of the art," then a mini-transgression
floods in like a nice formal device, someone we bit
when we were a "couple" who now we remember as we rub
lotion on ourselves, home alone, in front of the TV
soaking strawberries in champagne. Relative newcomers
to this part of the country, we feel we can "catch up"
by monitoring the culture in general, seeing what

in particular is different about our new base. Mind you,
we have no intention of "seeing ourselves" in anyone,
but as we refer more and more to our condition as "the surface,"
we have a fear of needing that world, which weighs an amazing ton

and is therefore truer than any symbol, a blazing faceless
instant pressed, as it were, to our lips, threatening
because of our ability not to have to live it

in order to remember. Once you see it played, it's "yours,"
so to speak. This scares us, an everpresent reminder
of limits, a physically perfect world gone to splinter.
The kind of thing that "turns heads" and "stops traffic,"
the model who knows he's gorgeous and can guarantee

he's never been in love, at least not the way we know
love, but rather is "from the place,"
and can infer the wind from the rain, from someone's hands
how long it's going to last, how someone's lips are going
to swell from the feeling really soon, this person
so devoted to self and life is beginning to be an audience
and in no way responsible. Personally speaking, we all
have a spirit that makes it easier to signal with a flame,
and we have a heart that makes it necessary for us to stop
for fresh cherries roadside, but beyond that,
we're indistinguishable from a world filled
to suffocating with "emotion." One touch is like another

as we see it, and the adjustment we made
back there is the one now seen as "perfect" for us then
and "perfect" for someone else now. In fact, we can see
someone doing what we did, watch it cost
what it cost then, we can embrace it fully as "ours," but are we
seeing ourselves or the thing we've made of ourselves,
and are we the same? We say it's getting light out
but cannot say it's late. We seem to be saving
for years for a rug at the foot of the bed, planting the last
marjoram on a balcony in California, but are we enjoying
a false immortality of imagery, the splendor
of moonlessness overlooking a sea?

164

The Butane Egg

Where once I hummed like a metropolis,
after I saw the bodies there was this feeling
of living in a foreign country, heated and
sealed like a humid summer day, one door away,
the one blown off, and in the middle
of the bridge – where we put it – two huts
painted green. My eyes.

                       My mind wasn't normal,
the sacrifice grew bigger because we feared admitting it,
like having a husband for a minute.
                 Why that feeling has vanished I don't know.
It was a small photograph. I suppose that makes us
               every reason to start with.

The future is a gesture that stimulates
the central nervous system – a new lyricism –
as much theater as you or me,
as once public TV was our projection,
now with an instant's notice
we are each other's project.

Among the few we one day came home bare
to sit by the brazier until the muddy smell
and shell shrunk in a classic calm.
Every time we stand up it seems a toy boat
tips to the left.

           – I've been waiting for you.
           – I'm always floating toward that crooked smile
                         on your face.

Will you be jealous if I tell you about this valley,
about being older, more dead, clearer
in memory? Our brakes squeal
without looking at the accident.

                    It's not as if lying in an open
hydrocarbon – the only really feminine thing in my life –
replaces several years in the life of a city.
Cities end like rivers running onto sand.

                    Our river –
the umbilical out of the valley –
                              is a copper wire.
On waking, the fuse is irretrievably lit.
Before chronic electricity, we were the ones
who loved the sun most –
now with the last bridge secured
to a dot, the August moon,
                         everyone's amphetamine
                    is a complex intent.

The Impossible

I had to give a great speech to a filled hall, beginning
with a flute sonata, and to recite from several books
only two of which I recognized,

which I accomplished, though it took everything out of me
as I tried to hold my posture erect and, failing that,
at least look good on the balls of my feet – this being
nearly impossible, I tried to give the illusion

of weightlessness, or at the very least a sense of rapprochement
with gravity, whereby my head remained light while my heart
suffered and my soul burned,

so that when asked to run, run for all I was worth,
which I tell you was not much by then, because of the pressure
to demur to those around me, cajoling and demanding,
I fled with a kind of verve even I did not foresee
since I was preoccupied with having abandoned a project
it's true only a genius or a madman might have finished
and which I had, frankly, more or less accomplished
by accident, intuition, and a sudden burst of confidence
which shocked even my dearest,

and succeeded in reaching the famous Crystal Springs
heretofore thought to be imaginary, a thing of wonder
but without substance, without substantiation, such blueness
and liquidity, it was unbelievable, but true,
that I stopped on a dime, resisting a personal moment
that surely would have overwhelmed anyone so haunted and

so driven by so many, and experienced what can only be described
as a disappointment, plain and simple, not because the waters
were any less majestic, any less transparent than rumored,

in fact, blue beyond the cerulean of sky over a south
high in the mountains of deepest earth, purpled, nearly black,
that is, if one thought of the sun ever going down
into such waters,

sad because I had never been more in love, more given over
to any one person, place, or thing, and all of existence
seemed paltry next to such feeling, if one did not count
the few stones that uncannily caught my eye, pebbles I
almost smashed out of a euphoria that overcame and nearly
destroyed me – a taste of heavenly winds swept my narrow body,
tickling my ribs with a fancy singing of spirit, tempting,
perfumed – but for the damned six or seven loosely strewn

aforementioned ugly little rocks that buckled my knees
with their gray snaky surface, pimpled, rough, impossibly
connotative, i.e., I saw a thousand lakes in the landscape
of a bird-shat mossy clump glommed to a crag, and bat faces
and bear paws and exoskeletal histories from beyond time,
and so on,

which held me face down, less recalcitrant than I had ever
been, trust me on that, and evermore eager to obey, the longer
I picked out lunar hills and valleys and the more hushed I got
between one ancient, practically moribund, megalith and another,
beamed, so to speak, from oblivion, the body of universe opened
into a gaping mouth

whose lips mercifully shined with the handiwork of creation, or
at least seemed that way to me, by now flattened to the cold

damp floor, reddened with the liveliness of movement, and of
sweat, crimson then, and moving, mouthing something, speaking
in tongues but almost immediately my language, words

I once dared to call, I grant you in a dream, the language
of love, which in this case hastened to particularize itself
in the being of a face, and then the hair and eyes and costume
of beatific figures transsexualized

by ritual and political charioteering such that I no longer
knew myself but rather a consortium of likenesses whose cocksureness
is colloquialized as immediately as the words for it are spoken –
a roaring of motorcycles and then hundreds of faceless, because
one face, hermaphroditic moderns blazed by, upstaging the mono-
chromatic past with theatric mauves and chartreuses, white-faced
and mascaraed images, eyebrowless, and I found myself in full
color, reproduced electronically, as it were, so eroticized
as to be unreal,

a diorama o'erpowering everything else in common limelight –
dykes on bikes, fag hags, drag queens, steroidal buffs, midnight
blue black semi-nudes, boytoys, unzipped sado-masochistic
six-foot tricks, the semi-erect, the innocent, in gym shorts
and in slips, tuxedos, T-shirts and cut-offs, jeans impaled
at the crotch – godly, larger-than-life meaning assigned
to them by messages spelled out on their chests, "Silence
Equals Death," etc., until, so engorged, their numbers blur
into a mass of energy that finally disperses into the missions
and the tenderloins from whence they came, into the planetary
city named irreverently and made familiar by necessity,
"sex,"

and I passed out onto those innocuous stones, trifles
I might have missed another day, waking to stumble

between two destinations, home or on, knowing I
had forgotten – o alcatrazed face, betrayed,
abandoned! – more than any metaphor provided

because it too is ultimately betrayed and abandoned,
forgotten life because of this paper face, this alphabet
and these blanks I trusted, naturally, like a form
of breathing, life I have to return to which I made

more difficult than walking off the globe
by imagining I had to say a few tired words
into an ear, near-empty auditorium...beginning
with a couple of scratched notes, only some of which
I'd actually written...

The General's Briefing

Here is the infant formula plant
missed by a hair's breath next to it
here is the biological research facility
bombed with advanced machinery
of pinpoint accuracy

Here are the small women and large babies
the medium-sized women with tiny children
and the large, the tall women with shrinking babies
and here are the former apartments and the former
neighborhoods and here is the dirty famous polluted well-known
historically besieged important river that ran
the commerce, throbbing in the belly of the city

Here are the candlesticks of the mosque
here are the pre-dawn musicians
here is dawn
here is the all clear
here are the radio waves
here are the telecommunication antennae
here are the rats
here are the fires
here is the dysentery
here is the one doctor
here is the vial of medicine for the population
here is the international community to rebuild the city
here finally is the city the dry faucet the endless alloy pipe
the rose plume over the scarlet plume
over the yellow plume over the charcoal over the flames

Here is the eyewitness
here are his notes his swollen pad
here his toothmarked lead pencil
his press pass his signature

here are the letters of his whole name
here are the vowels separating from the rest
here the tender "e" the demanding "u" the sorry "o"
and the "a" and "i" suddenly very close intimate in fact
given the circumstances of no air no water no electricity
no society no geography no say no information no

here is the audience the couch soiled the telephone
wired to the living room the Super Bowl on TV
the background of epic winter sky the letters recycled
practice jets the speed of sound the traffic Sunday
shoppers with their imported and domestic cars
tuned to the war

the clerk at Circle K
tuned to the war
the anti-war demonstrators with their headsets
tuned to the war
the Super Bowl commentators making an exorbitant fee
tuned to the war
the police guarding the stadium
the FBI routing out possible terrorists
the boys growing mustaches to be terrorists
the terrorist feeling death's high

Here is the answer here is the Pope the minister the President
the representative of the people here is the student the official
here is the quarterback here is the servant here here

Monday night – don't you see us on the shelled road,
out of gas, without our masks, money, without our credentials,
we sense you, your eye on the high-tech telescope, as one
throws back his stringy hair from his forehead,
another rubs her throat, waking it – the only thing
missing from your screen, your vision, out of earshot
the smell of so-called immortal souls, immortal earth,
fruit ripened, ready for market,
baths ended abruptly, weeks ago, the last of the drinking water,
the only thing missing from your enormous awareness
the smell – as when one meets the great love of his life, the same
yellow hair she imagined the very same speech same touch same
upturned lips, and cannot –
the smell – as when one hears her child and cannot –
the smell – who has slept all night, the sheets cold & wet –
the smell – silence suddenly, electronic, professional, governmental
silence –
the smell – whitewashed walls on all sides, infinite –
the smell – desert trenches, a face, a leg –
the smell – red hills, anxiety, our heads held up on sticks

as I speak from a third-floor room the smell
throughout the city the country the region
carnal diarrhea & vegetal puke & mineral dry heave
no salt for tears no sea for sewage –

Innocence

Fire on the mountain, fire under the lake.
Like children, we look on and dream.
We are loved, and none of the images
for love is absolute, so we are frightened.
We cast a glance into our past,
and not at any remarkable affair
but ordinary efforts – that spray of light
at breakfast where we ran out of milk –
we feel as somehow true.
Dare we touch it with a word
it loses its meaning, though not
its beauty. It becomes a fire
in the heart, incomprehensible and expressive,
an image of the whole, so that when finally a man
falls in love with life, it is like an arbor
begged of a desert, for he has accepted
the mirage. Now he is filled with goodness,
as if the unknown were something somehow
slightly slowed, a whole world
in one mountain, pool, and sky
under which we sit sipping milk.
So we are twelve again,
our sexual experience of the world focused
on that tree under which we undress.
The willow caresses us with a sudden gust,
but we have already turned, made up our mind.
It's very cold in the mornings, and hot by noon.
Plants grow slowly and never die completely.
Nowhere is there greater sympathy

than between the porcelain sky
and the chlorinated waters of the pools.
Still it stays with us that at any moment
a miracle might enter us as easily.
For we are lucky, we are children
in their fullest expression – lonesome
because we are moving through time
like a dot that becomes a sleeping figure
who is actually dead,
who has been killed,
and from whose nightmare
we continually wake into another
world, a moment we feel like kissing
someone's half-open mouth, once only
an image of fire and water.

New Body

There's a sort of eternity
when we're in bed together
whether silently you awaken
me with the flat of your hand
or sleep breathing with a small scratch
in your throat, or quietly attach
a bird to the sky I dream
as a way in to my body –

Now you have made me excited
to accept heaven as an idea
inside us, perpetual
waters, because you let yourself
fall from a sky you invented
to a sea I vaulted
when it was small rain
accumulating – My heart drained

there and fills now in time
to sketch in the entire
desert landscape we remember
as an ocean port,
that part of me accepting
your trust, a deep
voluptuous thrust into my hours,
that has no earthly power

but lives believing you were made for me
to give in to completely,
every entry into you the lip

of water that is in itself scant hope
broken into like sleep
by kisses – Policed in the desert
by a shooting star, we are the subversive
love scratched out of sky, o my visitor.

With the World

I would like to finish
a computer project, or one stinking letter
for work, or menu for lunch,
even before that,
to get to market
as they unload tomatoes –
organic, from Nogales – nowhere
sweeter for January, young, fleshy.

I would like to convince an acquaintance
I am better now that the drama
between me and my lover is over,
a truce, if I may say so,
regarding our long-standing feud.
We shook in a restaurant, that is, we cried,
and cut the fish, forcing a lemon.
A pity, we said, we were still eating
from the sea, not quite like slaughtering
a cow, but nonetheless obscene.
Then we paid too much,
saying it was worth it.
Later I thought about worth,
and couldn't finish, the phone sounded
and the sky split with practice jets
despite the distance of the war
around a corner of the globe.
A meteorologist swelled one in her hand
on the TV – I had her on "mute" –
as meanwhile I failed to persuade

my acquaintance – of anything, in fact –
hanging up on her, inside, shut tight,
registering the report on winter desert
weather, dry and hot, very dry and hot, not
at night, at night the unexpected daily cold,
again dry, cold dry winds, a little
dry, cold, sandy, empty wind.

Next the reporter from the front,
that desert very much
like mine in Tucson, where they train,
dry and hot, then at night, generally
quiet, cold. The picture punctuates
with Scud fire and Patriot interception,
except when the American system fails
and the Russian system (categorically
no longer the enemy), lights
the sky, the apartment building
cinder slightly bluer on cable TV.
Or am I imagining seeing the attack,
seeing the attack the next day? A dry
voice crackles, garbled like a forties evening
over radio waves, a nasal traditional
Hebrew song droning without instrument,
strangely pagan and Appalachian, a cry
rattling in the cavity of a dulcimer,
like an empty, once lived-in apartment.
(If only I could remember the story,
the year?, _____ goes out for some pears,
with only her purse and a cardigan, a
little dress, gets picked up by Germans and never
returns again, lands up in Israel, no one
has heard of her, a poet, somebody's lover).

I would like to finish listening
to the war, to sit alone another hour
with my aging remote and follow
updates from the leaders of the free world,
ours, of course, and from them
infer advice – it's not impossible – about
my life, the casualties of love,
albeit the analogy is damned inappropriate,
I cannot help a personal moment, petty, yet
I would like to finish the narrative,
or at least be allowed to go back, perhaps
merely for lunch, having shopped outdoors,
the weather perfect, cool late into morning,
sealed my exemplary work into envelopes,
quarreled, turned my acquaintance
into a friend, yes, to be able to return,
burst a couple of tomatoes – a happy accident–
while confiscating the best, young, fleshy,
only a little purple, bruises I can accommodate,
practically deny if I turn them underside.

Creon decrees that Polynices, who led an attack
against the city, shall be left unburned,
"carrion for the birds to tear,
an obscenity for the citizens to behold."
Outside the city, pecan and lemon trees
wait for rain – rain would be untimely,
but they know nothing of that –
it happens, bad weather, reconnaissance
can't make out the damage to the front.
Oil fields on fire, lemons in fog,
which drop onto dead-of-night moss,
gone by dawn. One picks his teeth,
thinking he's off-camera.

Coupling

Adolescent Bacchus in his grape wreath lies semi-
sheathed in front of a bowl of figs, grapes, pears,

apples & a loose peach, & his eyebrows are penciled in
for all the world to see he is a god & real, sexy,

muscular & with a summer paunch, late summer, patches
out a window of hay & green fields what he is

perhaps looking at, so unchanged is the scheme & always
drawn to human scale, posing in a dank basement to get

the shading right, so the summer is all in his dark
round eyes: if your silken skin can stand

another bite, plump evening, it will not show on his body,
his right nipple left of center so nearly perfect we are

mirrored there; Art fusses & the pool of wine in the hand-
blown carafe won't blink, nor will his offer of a taste

held out to you change you in the head, because in fact
he may be showing you what he's about to sip & never

share; I hate to think what you are doing now, over there,
gone from me as distantly as a century in a world that lifts

its taboos more easily than we ever wanted to
lift my body off of you, in other words, never, typically

a day & night, my idea about love misshapen into a sound, no,
into an argument or a story I forget, I've had a rough night

with the power cut, hours of pounding in a bowl of mountain
thunder, eyeballing this medieval town illumined by the oldest

trick in the book, God's theatrics like a drunk lit from within
coursing a way home across the pitched sky; a blessing

upon your sun-drenched August morning, your former furnace-
blasted city gone middle management into computer lines

while I prepare to leave my own adopted alien culture, a
burning reduced to a smell inside a memory inspired

by a word like "hay" or "sunflower" & not the other
way around, as Proust thought – it starts in the abstract

& races to the heart like lightning to an apple bough
in a pastoral, love, a scene, darling, wherein one person

cuts into another with a disdain borne out of the past
& recreated in the present as if it were real, causal,

a subject open to criticism, interpretation, theory, preference;
so you hate me now too, as then

in a sweaty room so electrified together we had to be
shouldered out of that world, black & blued

to be spared a fire whose flame tips came
too close to the truth: our father who art

in heaven & not in his right bed
puts out the cigarette & tires of his glory; now that you are free

& have done with me without so much
as lifting a finger & I imagine

happier for it, red buttocked by the lake of your youth
where it is safe to say we were a nightmare, a match

in a haystack, it is here meanwhile they've had to plant
the ubiquitous sunflower for the oil lost during a freeze

of their famed olive groves, a country brought to its knees
making of woe a supplication & a remedy; they say

Caravaggio killed somebody & anyway was a pagan & a homo-
sexual; if you put a coin in a metal box a twenty watt bulb comes on

for five minutes in a cold corner of a church & up rises one
of his portraits tourists in a dozen languages crush in

to view until the light cuts & no one budges, massed in the
cave staring at the eye socket which remains; someone then

has to cough up the change or forget about it, it's always
the same, too cheap or stupid, too passive, until some lame

bystander catches on, & the burning lasts forever for another
five minutes, all eyes tortured to the wall, the characters

that live on the wall, in the paint, in a stable or
what have you, a reflection of universal law; they seem real,

stopped forever proffering red wine in the lake
of some long-stemmed glass, say, with a crown of late summer

purplish grapes & autumn leaves; an adolescent
with a woman's face & a man's boyish hairless chest,

a killer perhaps, & certainly a drunk & a queer or whatever,
just the same, someone somebody or some several

knew intimately, by the stained teeth & weathered hair,
so real you could lick the flesh like a cat

daydreaming over cream with a thoughtless expression,
like when you're thinking or think you're thinking

about those too distant to be made out coupling in a field
of freshly-mown hay, a thousand eyes of sunflowers on them.

Cast from Heaven

There must have been something like writing across their faces.
There would have been sorrow, and tenderness, would there not?
And a sound, as if someone, I don't know by what means, spoke
our first thoughts upon waking.
We won't see them again, vagrants, skins.
A rash of daylight.

Careful. Time pairs with nature,
time is evil and sentimental.
One vital expression will return you to the creamery for your fill
and it will be farther and farther away,
no longer part of the country but deep in the bowel
of the city, which is all but framed in memory.
A few spires, girders extended into space,
and beyond, sky, where the sun stamped everything for deportation.

Once there was a choice, to talk or not, to boast,
to stall, we accepted it; but now, cast from heaven
the few words correspond only to ideas, and cannot help us
spend the night. Here's a man,

let's watch him and learn what he thought,
separated from his child, who chose her mother
when there was no difference.
He said, *God,* and it sounded
like *what?*
and like *stop.*
We mustn't let go the mother and child simply
because they wished to point at the sky.
What is the sense at the end?

The greasy soap bubbles where the creamery drained into a lake,
the grease-spot of the lake into the sky.

We sit around the fire.
Military terminology, slang, specific reference to
recent books, a grunt – those awake
meditate on the long night
while the sleeping dream dawn.
Thus work and rest are shared.

Marin Headlands

Grief as we know it
and pity as we know it,
the roaring foggy darkness as we know it,
love as we know it
and beauty and magnetism,
energy, as we know it,
as we have come to know it,
relationship and intimacy, as we know,
the great earthquake, life, as we know it,
tension, destiny, family,
movement at the subtlest level of function, as we know it,
human beings as we know them,

California, the blue dolphin,
the eucalyptus, the umbrella pine, the coastline,
as we have come to know them,
the mist, the lovers, the children,
the aging, the homebound, the irreversible,
these, as we have come to know them, the homosexual's parade,
the mayor's limousine, the homeless's cape of newspaper,
as we call them, our plate of food our rings our fresh haircuts
our meager donation our writers our poetry, as we have come to know it
our education our manner our estate our transportation our travel
our privacy our privilege as we have come to know it our sexuality
our vision as we know it

lightning as it is known, plants, peaches, wine,
failure, esteem, faith,
the future, as it is known, the noun,
as we have come to know it,

a "thought" as we know it, a "commitment" a "vote" a "religion"
as we know them,
ghosts, tempests, gods – the days, the instances,

the dream, as we know it, the poetic, the pacific, the allegorical,
the excuse, as we know it, the error,
the meaning, as we have come to know it, far away,
as we have come to know it, death, as we know,
heaven as it is known, and timelessness and grace, as is
expected to know, and as we have come to,

loathing, avarice,
a drink, a safety net, a parent, a dog, a weapon, a
response, a paddle, a marine, a debutante, a quarter,
a parasite, without knowing it, a minor actor, a case in point,
a husband, a weekend, without knowing, an admission,
a clue, without knowing, a country, a pope,

land rights, tenants, garages, inventory,
without knowing them, a twenty-seven year old, without knowing it,
it, itself, them, themselves,
as we know without knowing

private parties with ribs barbequed, embroidery of dead names,
the state of Russian music, the modern sensibility, as it is known,
the telecommunications network, the criminal element, as they are
known, the "wall," the "bomb," the "communist," the "TV," the "free,"
as they are variously known
and now me, without knowing, as is generally known,
me, as the sea and sky appear to know without knowing,
and you, knowing full well, without knowing,

"plump girls pinched with butter," "babies with roses and baby roses,"
January, February, June and July,

lipstick and blood, as they are associated and known,
as we have come to know our home, our place, our time, our
hour, our
favorite,
dark beach as we have come to,

in agreement, with little else to say, as a matter of course,
silenced, not a moment too soon, without further ado, without
a word in edgewise

the mere mention of three in the afternoon, a Tuesday in summer,
memories, as they are variously known
and were to have been understood and, commonly, forgiven,
this choice and those images and that situation
and this conclusion,
these approximations and those generalizations, as we know
and fear them,
as is our nature, toothy, hairy, spiny,

a faultline of carmine poppies, raspberries,
spring green gullies, grasses
and ravens,
a place never seen, the imagination as we know it,
bugless and treeless and airless and waterless and sunless.

By Nature

If it could be, it would be seven o'clock.
Two men who have all day
been picking peaches and pears
go back through the rows
for the fallen and pecked fruit
left for dead.
They take them for themselves,
filling the wire baskets of their motorbikes.
They light cigarettes
and pedal their engines to a running start.
Then an unexpected thing.
It cannot even be said
the sun resists setting –
in itself still something –
the sky behind it so recently
darkening "brightens"
but only by my recollection.
I surprise myself
with an angry thought
I'm as far away as you
make me, you shit
about my lover,
whom I had until this moment
the option of missing.
When I understood my being
half a globe away,
I assumed I could get there in time.
The earth is now
like a fruit a human
has knifed,

tumbling fruitlessly
through space.
You notice when you finally stop
running through your day,
at table, the dizziness,
the blown earth in the red wine.
And the constant
bruising as we fall up,
like falling out of love
where you are suddenly free,
terribly guilty
without caring.
No longer is there a single self
but a whole host
of opposition, completely random
pellets and debris,
mistresses and masters of the universe,
who will be there for you I promise, always.

Desert Abstract

It might have been a little different,
                              your hair auburn or brown, longish,
torn about by a rip-wind,
                              high tide, the muffled pounding deafening,
an explosion in a pillow
                    emblazoned on my face like
a like a lie invading a smile
                    blood coming in on a northeaster,
                                        our steamy souls
destined for the plates of gods,
                    an indestructible hour
of suffering like gods
                    after they have eaten and been surprised
by their slaves and skewered
                    screaming "history now" "destiny now"
everyone wanting a little quiet
                    in the end, a kind of reserve
following the buck and resound
                              of our finally pouring our hearts out,
                    our wharf rats and moon slag hosed down
                         for white space
which regrets nothing
                    is not guilty
                              and reprimands the violets
we hydrate by whispers by real feelings by tears,
                    showering a desert on eternity

Poetry

Invited onto the grounds of the god,
who decides what words mean,
we are amazed at the world
perfect at last. Gold fish, gold finches, gold watches,
trash blasted into crystal, all
twilights supporting one final sunset
with slender fingers of consolation.
A little reality goes a long way,
far off in the distance the weak sea
beaches its blue whales, the small sky
melds the stars into one
serious fire, burning eternally
out of control, our earth.
But here we are visiting
the plutonium factory dazzling
to the eye, the one good one remaining
to us in our wisdom. We have concluded
that automatic, volcanic sunrises and sunsets
where light trips on the same cardboard vine
are blinding, and we would rather fail
painfully slowly than survive a copy
of the world perfect at last. Yet we are
impressed by the real thing, which we walk
like dew upon flesh, suddenly lubricated and translucent
beyond our dreamiest desires, hard-pressed
to object. Consoled that there is so little
difference between the terrible and the real,
we admire the powerful appleseeds bobbing
in the dewy pools, we cannot help
but enjoy their greeny spring, and it is only by resting

on the miraculous grass, wildly uniform, mildly serene,
that we sense
with our secret selves, the little bit we left behind and
remember, that we are out of our element, that we are
being made into words even as we speak.

Adoration

Now I have come from the Berg String Quartet Opus 3
performed by the Young Artists of the Taos School
home in a sperm of rain
that declares itself to the loaded fireplace
as dead as the world last Friday
though God knows there is a drought in every other state
we live by voices we shall never hear.

May the violent haystack consuming himself as a young man
(that night I went misshapenly to witness the Los Angeles Lakers)
be eaten off the table by the broadening sun
and not the barkeep who bloodies the evening steak.
He was not soundlessly spilling his Miller
onto a manufactured Mexican teen, but I saw and was
hoarse by the time he will reach her alarm

under the stars' neon shoes, stepping lightly over the firmament
of Oglivie's where the plane trees yellow the margaritas
of the yellow moon behind them, and the brown moon of rain drowns
the elbow moon of that face coming closer to crumbling
before we can choose, before we can announce there is a choice,
before we can prove there is, there was.
I have a handle on my jeans where I would provide

that turn in the town where the tourists meet the art trade
for the firewood they will burn next winter
while skiers fly overhead in an enforced frieze,
a bride a minute beholding Agua Fria Peak in her Angel Fire
T-shirt, while her husband ejaculates from an Air Force jet,

where once there were a few now many,
once a hundred now a state of collapse, a couple of

dogs who pitch and yaw all night for a little water.
For now is the opening the art world belittled, the V-neck and
the bedspread, the stockinged leg, the chain and gear
makeup, the turquoise that lights the lights of the lights
that are lit, our souls nippled with antennae so the world will
hear, the party will know we were the ones who trained like mad to
do it, do it, do it in the perforated gleam of the dollhouse window.

Sonnet Against Nuclear Weapons

The human sigh commuted to life imprisonment –
it's a sparrow in the hazels and pines.

A log, and so on and so forth,
anti-pastoral and realistic.

There was a dinner, you can see for yourself,
clean napkins, it might have been far worse,

entering a lit room undressed;
an unlit room, dressed.

It isn't anything you want to think about.
And went pale.

With a stranger for the first time in her life.
With a stranger for the first time in the afterlife.

The light in the room on both of them.
I'm writing on the back of a child's drawing,

a snake. Slightly protruding belly, creamy,
round breasts. Sometimes when I think of her

she remembers. Seven eyes of God
play the tape forward a little, stop it, replay it.

The phone's ringing in someone else's place.
– I'll get it.

When she thinks of moving tonight,
the seven eyes of God in the hazels and pines

enter an unlit room, a little
pale on the back of a child's drawing,

slightly protruding belly, and realistic.
It might have been far.

She remembers a human sigh against
the suppression of rights. A snake.

Art History

This hidden hag whose face belies the young face in front
                         is a shrine completely open
                                        so it's possible to observe
the image of the goddess from any angle, this new day

a face torn off; features now bunched together, scattered over
the battleground, a melancholy of alterations
                         for which language has only physical
                                        analogies –

                         her twist of mouth not so
dead that it cannot
(nothing spared) faceted, folded & twisted, hard like a wrench
not heal –

– We made it,
                                        hurtling
out of indulgence & not the other way around,
                         tossed heads of gorged horses:

then we broke up;
                         the foreshortened depths
of the turns, & bit my nipple on the way out of her
life, the inside of a pleated bellow,
                         measured spans, slopes & hollows.

                         The gods had been busy on & off for days
when they asked a question of perspective as to whether
(strike the man entering the salon of a brothel with a faun, a chair, & a
                                        bowl of fruit)

the beast in the lady is the back of her head
                              or her lover's hand.

                              It took everything to get her up in the morning
& out of the house
                              strewn urns, chairs, Japanese panels, & loosed
                                                            over the goddamn
desert floor
                              (put x-rated after)
the recumbent sleeper with both arms overslung,
                    the sleeper prone, belly to ground, cheek resting on arms,
a space filled with wonder, surety, desire, respect, daylight
& dark periods
                              such that everything exactly reversed
                                             is unbelievable & true,

the female nude's double pomes,
                              buttons & clefts, my darling,
mosquitoes on her, a harvest; a ruin.

Countryside

My darling works until she finishes   I resist starting –
            craning out the upper window over the tiled roofs
we each imagine the moon sets in night mist
            she says she sees it I pretend I don't

over our heads someone who makes a lot of money
            does something arty the public likes like pouring color
over red cherries –
            not delicious wrong language

when she finally finishes I am in the kitchen again
            counting supplies wondering if we can return
neither thinks we've woken from a strange dream
            I'd gotten to the bottom of a sensation

tied up with doing nothing until I felt
            one way or the other in other words nothing
and then being blown away by relationship never helps
            – did you do that? No you made me –

it's all I can do to clean up from the night before
            light streaming off the ancient stones
small windows for defensive purposes the whole village set on a slope
            the quest was for a form that wouldn't sacrifice presence

the answer Picasso is said to have given the German officer
            who asked pointing to *Guernica* did you do that? No you did that
it amounts to some ulcerated nights some tangled hair
            beautiful old bottles nets

songs before the sun is up

   not proscriptive but love all the same

such that I find I would never talk to anyone

   whose day doesn't last a month or a year

in town shopping we stop for soup

   the canopy's shoved back there are stars for everyone

& get home drunk

   hoping the bread soaks the burn

mornings I read my tourist book

   ape the population rather than look American

when will I wise up?

   very warm & pleasant birds despite the heat

we make love waiting to stop the spin by hand

   or the wash charges up again

someone drops by to see the kitchen made from the ruin

   this regular stuff emerges as an image

something scary something to hurt us

   to make us dead

& art –

   she never wakens me so when I'm awake I'm unguarded

could it be relationship & not matter with whom?

   as easily as this sky be a diagram & not an embrace

same sky different death's head behind it

   small jar of anchovies olive oil & salt

Foundered Star

Little fevered island, blued to closing,
boatmen, tidemen, shademen, men of color
and of peace;

women of the cabbage, women of the carrot-house,
women of the swim;
children squealing and picnicking, doe-eyed
and able-bodied, children of clashing cymbals and chalky
dreams, of milk-lips, of bugs under glass;

come now to the tips of the roofs, come now to the lake
lip, to the entryway of the tunnels, to the counting-house;

air the eiderdown, steam the rooms of the lovers, break
the fistfights from their arguments, marry the maid –

live a little in the afternoon, asking,
                        – now what do I do?

because this is the way we are alive, though we force ourselves out
of a certain nostalgia, where we first made love
the condition of our lives –
                        a dark room there, but only because
the shades were drawn, it was really midday!, and our clothes stuck
to our bodies like hairy beasts! – we watched the light change
in our eyes, as we dug deeper, pulling out embers –

remember? But the word itself is no longer magical,
the word no longer a living thing…a weakness in one of two breakers.

Yet there remains an image, when you water the sun and moon, mouths
coupling and uncoupling, kissing along the ridge the poet
invented, coincident, temporal, carnal, all
so that others might be entertained, changed a nick or two
like a diamond. Who can say whether better or worse, but this much
I can say, I who am always writing

                                        to you, my earthship, my

next life –
though no one is now
listening or talking (it's all the same)
though no one is now
laboring or sleeping (it's forbidden)
no one yet exploded, the globe forgives
the night sky gone yellow, the morning sea gone white
and all for a little greed, a little light on the wall,

a view of the other side – oar dipped in ink! –
where we shall never again believe things
about ourselves that aren't true.

The Enchanted Forest

That nothing intercept
the burning of our fates,
as sweet as an orchard

may we stand in the nude tiger-eyed
rather than be provided
an umbrella from the sun,

piercing the deaf-to-a-thousand-stories
the day after a war,
a cold-stopping chill

in the heart of a people.
Let us board up
like a hundred windows

giving onto hell
the material body of our message,
the joy in true contact

with things, merciful things,
the very bonds of an idiot society,
and stand on our last pivot,

a magnificent move, a steady, untoward
mountain of a move, and speak
in a straightforward manner

with the least important
least visited, raped, riddled
speech in nature,

no,
not from your balcony,
not outside your door

or within,
but to death's own
homesickness

speak with our eyes down on
the sex of our loved one
no one's name,

let no one out of clay and earth
grieve rain's rainbow,
love, alone,

yet say the face through the back of the head,
the front of a unicorn from behind,
horsing, shining – ...

JANE MILLER was born in New York and currently lives in Tucson, where she is on the faculty of the Creative Writing Program at the University of Arizona. She is the author of *Working Time: Essays on Poetry, Culture, and Travel* (University of Michigan Poets on Poetry Series, 1992) and several earlier volumes of poetry, including *The Greater Leisures*, a National Poetry Series selection, and *Black Holes, Black Stockings*, a collaboration in the prose poem with Olga Broumas, as well as two other volumes from Copper Canyon, *American Odalisque* and *August Zero*, which won the Western States Book Award. She has received a Lila Wallace–Reader's Digest Award, a Guggenheim Fellowship, and two Fellowships from the National Endowment for the Arts.

BOOK DESIGN & COMPOSITION by John D. Berry & Jennifer Van West, using Adobe PageMaker 6.0 on a Macintosh IIvx and a Power 120. The text type is FF Scala, designed by Martin Majoor, and the display type is FF Quadraat, designed by Fred Smeijers. Both typefaces are part of FontShop International's FontFont type library. Scala is a humanist typeface with an open character shape; it was created in 1988 for the printed matter of the *Muziekcentrum Fredenburg* in Utrecht, in the Netherlands, and released in 1991. Quadraat which displays the subtle irregularities of a handmade typeface, which give it a distinctive character at large sizes; it was released in 1992. The sans serif display type used on the cover is FF Dirty Seven Two, a "damaged" typeface designed by Neville Brody as part of the Dirty Faces 2 font package and released by FontShop in 1994. *Printed by McNaughton & Gunn.*